HARLEQUIN®
Presents

w/7F

In Harlequin Presents books seduction and passion are always guaranteed, and this month is no exception! You'll love what we have to offer you this April….

Favorite author Helen Bianchin brings us *The Marriage Possession,* where a devilishly handsome millionaire demands his pregnant mistress marry him. In part two of Sharon Kendrick's enticingly exotic THE DESERT PRINCES trilogy, *The Sheikh's Unwilling Wife,* the son of a powerful desert ruler is determined to make his estranged wife resume her position by his side.

If you love passionate Mediterranean men, then these books will definitely be ones to look out for! In Lynne Graham's *The Italian's Inexperienced Mistress,* an Italian tycoon finds that one night with an innocent English girl just isn't enough! Then in Kate Walker's *Sicilian Husband, Blackmailed Bride,* a sinfully gorgeous Sicilian vows to reclaim his wife in his bed. In *At the Greek Boss's Bidding,* Jane Porter brings you an arrogant Greek billionaire whose temporary blindness leads to an intense relationship with his nurse.

And for all of you who want to be whisked away by a rich man… *The Secret Baby Bargain* by Melanie Milburne tells the story of a ruthless multimillionaire returning to take his ex-fiancée as his wife. In *The Millionaire's Runaway Bride* by Catherine George, the electric attraction between a vulnerable PA and her wealthy ex proves too tempting to resist.

Finally, we have a brand-new author for you! In Abby Green's *Chosen as the Frenchman's Bride* a tall, bronzed Frenchman takes an innocent virgin as his wife. Be sure to look out for more from Abby very soon!

Kate Walker

SICILIAN HUSBAND, BLACKMAILED BRIDE

ITALIAN HUSBANDS

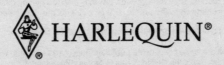
HARLEQUIN®

TORONTO • NEW YORK • LONDON
AMSTERDAM • PARIS • SYDNEY • HAMBURG
STOCKHOLM • ATHENS • TOKYO • MILAN • MADRID
PRAGUE • WARSAW • BUDAPEST • AUCKLAND

ISBN-13: 978-0-373-12622-4
ISBN-10:   0-373-12622-0

SICILIAN HUSBAND, BLACKMAILED BRIDE

First North American Publication 2007.

This edition published by arrangement with Harlequin Books S.A.

® and TM are trademarks of the publisher. Trademarks indicated with ® are registered in the United States Patent and Trademark Office, the Canadian Trade Marks Office and in other countries.

www.eHarlequin.com

Printed in U.S.A.

All about the author...
Kate Walker

KATE WALKER was born in Nottinghamshire, England, and grew up in a home where books were vitally important. Even before she could write she was making up stories. She can't remember a time when she wasn't scribbling away at something.

But everyone told her that she would never make a living as a writer, so instead she became a librarian. It was at the University of Wales, Aberystwyth, that she met her husband, who was also studying at the college. They married and eventually moved to Lincolnshire, where she worked as a children's librarian until her son was born.

After three years of being a full-time housewife and mother, she was ready for a new challenge, so she turned to her old love of writing. The first two novels she sent off to Harlequin were rejected, but the third attempt was successful. She can still remember the moment that a letter of acceptance arrived instead of the rejection slip she had been dreading. But the moment she really realized that she was a published writer was when copies of her first book, *The Chalk Line*, arrived just in time to be one of her best Christmas presents ever.

Kate is often asked if she's a romantic person because she writes romances. Her answer is that if being romantic means caring about other people enough to make that extra-special effort for them, then, yes, she is.

Kate loves to hear from her fans. You can contact her through her website at www.kate-walker.com or e-mail her at: kate@kate-walker.com.

For Lori Corsentino, who let me borrow her
brother's names for these books.

PROLOGUE

IT WAS the perfect day for a wedding. The sun was shining, with the promise of heat later in the day, but it was early enough that the slight coolness of the dawn still lingered.

At home in England the early flowers of spring would be blooming purple and gold and white, the trees newly covered in soft green foliage. But here in Las Vegas there were only the city streets and the high, high buildings where the glass of thousands of windows glinted in the morning sun.

But she didn't miss the green and the flowers, and colours of home, not for a second. She'd found a new home. She wouldn't want to be anywhere but here, right now, in this perfect moment.

Because today was going to be perfect, no matter what the weather or anything else was like. And she was totally, perfectly happy. She couldn't possibly find any space in her heart for any more joy or delight.

Today she was marrying the perfect man, the most wonderful man in the world.

Her mind was still spinning with the unexpectedness, the speed with which it had all happened. Just days before—not even a week ago—she hadn't even known that he existed. And then a chance meeting in a hotel lobby, a dropped handbag, had changed her life for ever. She had crouched down to pick up her belongings and someone—some man—had stopped beside her. A soft, beautifully accented voice had asked if he could help. A strong hand, the skin tanned golden brown, had reached down to her, and she had looked up into the most gorgeous pair of gleaming bronze eyes she had ever seen in all her life.

And lost her heart in the magical space between one beat and the next.

Impossibly, unbelievably, he had felt the same way too. From the moment of that first meeting they had been inseparable.

But marriage…

Marriage!

Laughter that was the result of pure happiness bubbled up in her throat then broke on a snatched-in breath as the cab pulled into the kerb and stopped.

She was here. She'd reached the little wedding chapel where they were to become man and wife.

It was white-painted and tiny. But, small as it was, it was more than adequate. After all, there would only be the two of them standing in front of the celebrant and the one witness required by law. What else did they need? What else but the love they had discovered so wonderfully, so unexpectedly here in this city so far from their homes?

And he was there.

It was only when she saw the tall, dark, devastating figure of the man she loved that she realised how much she had been holding her breath, never quite believing that it was going to happen. Men like him—beautiful, powerful, exotic men like him— didn't marry girls like her. She had been stunned enough that he had wanted her, had fallen into bed with him without even stopping to think if it was wise, so lost in love had she been. She hadn't thought of anything more, hadn't thought of a future then. She hadn't even dreamed of such a possibility. It had been just enough to be with him, to know him, to share his bed—to *love* him.

The car door was pulled open and he was there, dressed in a loose white shirt, black linen trousers and smiling the smile that had stolen away her heart in the first moment she had seen it.

'You came.'

'Of course I came.' The laughter and excitement were still a ripple in her voice. 'Did you doubt it?'

'Never,' he responded, his own voice low and deep. 'Not for a minute.'

Outside on the pavement, she waited while he paid the driver, her feet moving restlessly, almost dancing in her impatience, wanting to hurry, to go inside—to walk down that aisle and start this new stage of her life.

She was getting married…

'Ready?' he asked and held out his hand.

'Ready,' she assured him, putting her own fingers into his.

But still he hesitated, just for a moment.

'You don't have any flowers. Here…'

And he handed her a single glorious deep red rose on a long, graceful stem with all the thorns carefully pruned away.

'It's beautiful…' she breathed, lifting the flower to her face and letting the velvet-soft petals brush her lips. 'So beautiful.'

'But nowhere near as lovely as you.'

He made her feel beautiful when he smiled down at her like that, bronze eyes glowing with warmth. He made her forget that she hadn't had the time or the money to find anything special to wear and that her dress was only a simple white cotton sheath, sleeveless and supported by delicate shoestring straps, her shoes just soft leather sandals. But none of that mattered.

Nothing mattered except the two of them and the love they shared. A love that would give them a future together when she had feared that what they had was coming to an end. Feared that she would have to let this precious moment of time become just a glorious memory: that she would have to go back home to face her mother's cold-faced disapproval and her determination to find her daughter a 'suitable' husband.

'So—shall we get married?'

'Oh, yes—yes, please!'

She wouldn't let thoughts of her mother intrude, she told herself as they walked hand in hand down the short wooden-floored aisle. She wasn't going to let anything spoil this day—their day.

The words of the ceremony floated over her head as she kept her eyes fixed on the dark, stunning face of the man who was to be her husband. She still couldn't believe that he had ever asked her. That he had ever said those magic words.

She had been sighing at the thought that her time in Vegas was nearly up, that she would soon have to leave and head home. The thought of what was waiting for her there had clouded her eyes, drained her smile.

'Would you stay if I asked you to marry me?'

She could still hear the surprising casualness of his tone, the musical lilt of his accent.

He had been lounging back in bed as he spoke, his dark head supported on his hands, his tanned chest bare above the whiteness of the sheets, and she had spun round from where she had been standing by the window, eyes wide as she stared at him in disbelief.

'Did you say…? Oh, yes! Yes, please! But can we do it soon? Can we do it here—now—as quickly as possible?'

If they left it any longer might he have second thoughts, change his mind? Declare he'd only said it as a joke? Oh, please, please, let it not be a joke.

'Can we get married tomorrow? Just find a chapel here and do it?'

And so here they were, just as she had wished. In this tiny chapel with its vivid candy-pink and white colour scheme.

And this wonderful man, this stunning, handsome man, the

man she had adored from the very first moment she'd seen him, was actually going to be her husband.

Somehow she stumbled through her vows, her voice shaking. Her hand trembled as she held it out to him, her finger slightly raised to receive his ring, and he caught hold of it, held it firmly in the strength of his as he pushed the ring down onto it.

'I now pronounce you husband and wife.'

'We've done it!'

The words escaped her on another bubble of delirious laughter. 'We've actually done it.'

It was then that the full reality of what had happened hit home to her. She was married. Married to a man she had met less than a week before. She had vowed to love and cherish him to be with him for the rest of her life—'till death us do part'.

And yes, a tiny, shaken little voice whispered inside her head, yes, she loved him so, so much. So much that she couldn't wait to be his bride and had rushed down the aisle just as soon as she possibly could. She loved him—but did she really *know* him?

The ground seemed to lurch beneath her feet as she looked up into his face, saw those stunning eyes fixed on her, felt his hand tighten around hers.

'We've done it,' he said and there was a note in his voice that caught on a nerve, so that just for a second it felt as if the sun had gone behind a cloud.

But then he smiled down into her upturned face and the sun came out again, brilliant and clear and wonderfully, magically warm. And as he bent his head to take her mouth in a long, lingering kiss, she felt all her fear, the momentary doubt evaporate like mist before that sun.

She loved him and that was all that mattered. They had all the rest of their lives to get to know each other. This man and her life with him would be her future and each day would be more wonderful than the first.

Today was the start of forever.

CHAPTER ONE

IT WAS the perfect day for a wedding.

The sun was shining, the breeze was warm and soft, and all along the edges of the gravel path that led from the carved wooden lych-gate to the metal-studded door of the little village church the early flowers of spring were blooming purple and gold and white. In the trees, newly covered in soft green foliage, even the birds were chirping softly to each other.

It was the perfect day and the perfect setting for an elegant English country wedding.

But in Guido Corsentino's mind, nothing could be perfect about the wedding towards which he was heading, his long, savage strides covering the ground with furious speed. And the mood that gripped him was far from idyllic; totally at odds with the bright sunlight of the day, the relaxed and smiling attitude of the crowd that had filled the narrow country lane.

They'd gathered there to see all the friends and relations of the bride and groom arrive in gleaming fleets of chauffeur-driven limousines. They'd watched them emerge, the men in smart, tailored morning dress, the women looking like so many brightly coloured birds of paradise as they made their way through the small churchyard. They'd oohed and aahed at the sight of the bride, slender and beautiful in her white silk gown, the antique lace veil covering her pale face, arriving at the church almost exactly on time to meet her groom.

And now they lingered, chatting quietly as they waited for the newly married pair to emerge from the church, hand in hand, as husband and wife.

They hardly spared a glance for the tall, dark, handsome man who strode past them, his total concentration fixed on the weathered stone building ahead. The few who looked his way took him for just one more of the wedding guests, though his black shirt, black trousers and loose black jacket were much more relaxed than the formal frock coats and top hats of the earlier arrivals. And if they noted the hard, cold set of the expression on his stunning, strongly carved face they took it for simple irritation that he was late and that the ceremony had already begun without him.

The truth was that Guido Corsentino was exactly on time. He had planned his arrival at the church for one very precise moment, and that moment was just about to arrive. And when it did he would be ready for it.

Ducking his black-haired head so as to dodge the low arch of the wooden lych-gate, he marched up to the closed door of the church and came to an abrupt halt. A dark smile of grim satisfaction curled the corners of a wide, expressive mouth as he caught the faint sound of music and voices from the cool interior.

He couldn't have timed it better.

Pausing to fasten the single button on his jacket, straighten the cuffs of his fine black cotton shirt, he reached for the door handle. As his fingers touched it, his heart kicked once, hard and high, at the thought of what—of *who* he would see beyond it. A memory surfaced with a cruel stab and an added twist of something darker and more primitive low down in his body.

The memory of another wedding, another setting so very different from this one. Another time, another place…

The need to see her just once more warred savagely with the

need to walk away to never see her lying face again. But the real reason he was here, the reason he had travelled thousands of miles just for this, came back in a rush, stiffening his spine and hardening an already coldly savage heart. Almost fiercely his head came up, he flexed his broad shoulders. His dark head held high, he opened the door as little as possible, and slipped quietly inside.

The bride and groom stood at the far end of the long aisle, facing the altar, their backs to him. The groom was the tall, narrow-framed man he was expecting, his thin blond hair already disappearing to display a bald spot near the crown of his head. He wore the formal frock coat as if he was born to the part—at least, as much as Guido could see from his back.

Beside him, *she*—his bride—was tall too; tall and slender. A blur of white.

White! Something inside him rebelled savagely at the thought. Bile burned in his stomach, lifted to his throat, making him swallow hard in distaste.

'Amber…'

The name escaped him in a whisper of savage fury.

Luckily the choir was singing some hymn so that no one heard him. Everyone had their attention on the front of the church too, and hadn't noticed his arrival.

So they didn't see the way that his face set even harder, his lips twisting in anger and the bitter taste of disgust flooding his mouth with acid.

Amber Wellesley wasn't entitled to wear white. He had made very sure of that.

But perhaps she had lied to her new fiancé about that. Just as she must have lied to him about something else. Something much more important.

She had lied when she had said she loved him.

His dark bronze eyes focused on the woman in white who stood at the altar steps, totally unaware of his presence.

Now that his gaze had cleared again he could see how the wonderful glory of her chestnut hair was piled high on her head, fixed with ornate silver pins over which the delicate veil tumbled in a waterfall of gauze. He had once known how it felt to unpin those burnished locks, comb them loose, feel them tumble over his hands, his skin…

'*Dio mio…*'

Guido's breath hissed between his teeth as he muttered a curse to himself. Already his heartbeat had lurched, threatening his ability to breathe right. His mind was flooded with burning erotic images that were totally inappropriate to standing in a church, watching the subject of those imaginings preparing to marry another man. He mustn't think this way. Must not let his mind wander onto paths that would too easily distract him from his purpose.

With a brutal effort he dragged his thoughts back from the direction in which they were heading and clamped down on the wayward imaginings. Cold, calm control was what he needed now. He had to play this just right.

He was a few minutes early anyway. But that didn't matter. He had planned this for just the right moment. The choir was coming to the end of the hymn.

Folding his arms across his broad chest, he leaned back against the heavy wooden door and prepared to wait.

The church was full of the scent of flowers. The perfume from sprays of roses and lilies that spilled out from the ornate holders on each side of the altar, and from the arrangements of tight little rosebuds and lily of the valley that decorated the end of every pew, flooded the air thickly. Amber's senses swam with every breath she drew in, making her feel nauseous and faint.

It might have helped if she had been able to sleep the night before, or eat something this morning, but both rest and food had proved impossible for her.

Which was hardly surprising under the circumstances.

'Every girl has the right to feel nervous on the night before her wedding,' her mother had assured her. 'A little blusher will soon improve the look of those pale cheeks.'

And Amber had forced a smile, submitting herself to her mother's ministrations as Pamela Wellesley wielded the blusher brush, the mascara wand, with enthusiasm, then stepped back to view her handiwork.

'You still look a little wan,' she murmured, frowning as she did so. 'Really Amber, you seem as if you're about to leave for your execution, not your wedding. Is there something wrong?'

'No!' It was too fast, too vehement, and it made her mother's eyes narrow sharply.

'No second thoughts about Rafe?'

'No.'

Of that she was sure at least. Rafe was kind and gentle and had been a good friend to her. It was not his fault that there wasn't any great passion between them. It was not his fault he was not…

No—she wouldn't let that name into her mind. Not today, of all days.

'You haven't had a row—?'

'Oh, Mum, how could anyone ever have a row with Rafe?'

It would help if she didn't know only too well what was going through her mother's mind. It wasn't the thought that her daughter might actually have rowed with her prospective husband, the man she was supposed to love, that was really troubling her, but the thought of what might happen if the wedding was called off. The uncomfortable scandal that would follow, the embarrassment…

Pamela had lived for months on the prestige she had gained from the fact that her daughter was going to marry one of the St Clair family, and she would hate the way she would lose face if anything happened.

'No. You're right, it's just nerves.'

'Well, I know something that could help with that—a glass of something…some champagne…'

'No! Nothing—thank you, Mum.'

Amber forced herself to add the second part of her sentence, knowing that once again she had come so close to giving herself away. The note of near-panic in her voice had sounded so sharply in her own ears that she couldn't believe that Pamela hadn't heard it. But her mother could have no idea of just what memories she had stirred up, and if Amber wasn't careful she would risk raising questions she had no hope of answering.

'I'm fine, honestly,' she assured her mother. 'Or I will be when today is over.'

When today was over and all the memories she had tried to lock away could go back into the secret part of her thoughts where she had hidden them for the past year, until the plans for this very different day had dragged them out into her mind again. When she could put the past behind her for good, she hoped.

The sudden silence around her in the church jolted Amber out of her reverie, dragging her back to the present. The choir had stopped singing, the glorious sound of their voices dying away, and the priest stepped forward to begin the real heart of the ceremony.

'We are gathered here together to join this man and this woman…'

Amber found that her mouth had dried painfully and she had to swallow hard to relieve the tightness in her throat.

Could she really do this? Could she go through with this wedding, knowing that her heart wasn't truly in it? She was fond of Rafe. She loved him in a quiet, gentle way—in the way that good friends loved each other. And a year ago, he had helped her escape from the worst situation of her life.

But she could never give her heart to him as she had once given it to another man. Given it and had it ripped to shreds, the tiny pieces tossed back at her without a care. With only supreme contempt on his face.

No!

With a violent mental effort, Amber clamped down tight on the Pandora's box of memories she'd risked opening again. She was not going to let that happen. She was not going to let *that man's* name into her thoughts, into her world, ever again. He had ruined her life once and she had barely recovered from it. She was not going to suffer that way ever again.

That was why she was marrying Rafe.

Turning her head, Amber looked up into the face of the man at her side, surprised to find that he looked pale—as pale as she imagined she must look herself. His jaw seemed tight, his mouth compressed. But then, as he realised her eyes were on him, he glanced her way too, and flashed her a brief smile.

Immediately Amber felt some of the cruel tensions that had tightened her spine, twisting in her nerves, slacken and ease, and she slid her hand into his where it hung at his side. His skin was cool, his response muted. He just let her fingers rest in his. But that was Rafe's way. He made no major demonstrations of affection; they hadn't even slept together. He had said he was happy to wait and that was how Amber preferred it.

She would be OK with Rafe. Safe and secure. And that was all she wanted in life now. She'd known passion once and it had frightened her. It had turned her into someone she didn't recognise and she never wanted to see that person again. She'd left the dark days behind her and she was moving forward at last.

'If any person present knows of any reason why these two should not be joined...'

The priest intoned the words in a voice that made them sound so solemn, so ominous, that in spite of herself Amber felt a tiny shiver run down her spine. It was deliberate, she knew. The cleric was Rafe's uncle and he had joked with them before the ceremony that this was their last chance to back out; to escape the marriage vows.

'I'll wait a good while after I've said it,' he'd teased. 'Just to make sure that if anyone wants to say anything they can.'

'...then let him speak now...or forever hold his peace...'

There, it was said. The words were out. The challenge had been made and now they could continue with the wedding service.

No one would answer it. No one ever did. Amber had no idea just how many weddings she had attended in her life but at all of them those words had been spoken in one form or another and no one had ever stepped forward to 'speak now' instead of forever holding peace.

But still, there was always that long-drawn-out moment that seemed to go on forever. The awkward, rather nerve-racking moment when everyone paused and listened and waited...and no one ever spoke.

But everyone wondered just what would happen if someone did.

Of course, no one spoke this time. And Rafe's uncle beamed with delight and satisfaction as he drew in his breath to continue once again.

'In that case—'

'I do!'

The voice came so suddenly and unexpectedly that for a moment Amber was confused. They were the words she was expecting to hear—when she and Rafe made their vows—but not yet, not before they had been asked...

Had Rafe been so nervous, in so much of a rush that he had jumped the gun, plunging in to say the words that everyone knew were coming? Surely not now, not yet. Not without the prompt from the cleric first.

'Wait...' she began to whisper.

At least, she opened her mouth to try to say it. But then she realised that the words had come from behind, and not beside her, And there was something dreadful about the still-ness that had fallen over the entire church, about the way that there had been one sudden murmur of shock, abruptly choked off and leaving instead an appalled silence that reverberated inside her head like the after-effects of a vicious blow to her skull.

'I do,' the voice said again and there was no mistaking it this time. This time she caught the soft lilt of a musical accent that should have made the words sound beautiful, soft, enticing.

Instead they made her shiver with the ice-cold, soul-deep dread that came with recognition of that voice. The voice she had once loved to hear whisper her name or tease her softly.

The voice that could only belong to one man and he was the man she hoped she would never meet again. The man she most dreaded seeing in the entire world.

'What—?' Rafe seemed to have jolted out of his inexplicable trance, some of the tension leaving his body as he jerked his head around to see who had spoken. 'What are you—?'

But the man behind them didn't let him finish. Instead he interrupted Rafe, lifting his voice slightly and speaking in a harsh and dangerous tone that defied anyone to try to stop him.

'I do,' he said again, just to emphasise the fact. 'I know of a reason why these two should not be joined together in holy matrimony. Don't I, Amber?'

And it was that use of her name, the icy cruelty in it, the savage edge to the syllables that turned it into an accusation, a warning and a threat all in one that left her with no place to go; nowhere to hide. The only thing she could do was to face her tormentor head-on.

Look him straight in the face.

It took all the strength she possessed. Trembling, shivering, nausea churning deep in her stomach, she forced herself to turn, green eyes blurring badly as she tried to focus them on him.

He was bigger than she remembered. Bigger and darker and far, far more devastating.

Or was that just the way that he seemed to be in contrast to the mellow stone and wood of the interior of the church, the pale colours of the flowers? He was dressed in superbly tailored black from head to foot, shirt, jacket, trousers, black boots on the feet that were planted so firmly on the stone flags that lined the aisle. With his jet-black hair and gleaming bronze eyes he looked like nothing so much as the devil himself come to earth—and come to torment her.

'Amber?' he prompted harshly when she could only stand and stare, eyes wide, her trembling hands half-raised towards her mouth, not having the strength to complete the move.

The whole congregation had frozen too. Her mother, Rafe's family, every one of the wedding guests was sitting completely still in their seats, goggle-eyed at the scene unfolding before them.

Suddenly there was an unexpected flurry of movement to one side, distracting Amber and drawing her gaze for a second. A friend of Rafe's family, Emily Lawton, recently widowed and five months pregnant, had collapsed in a faint, sliding limply down from the pew to land on the stone floor.

But someone was already there to help her, and Amber's own impulsive movement was stilled by the way that Guido took a couple of steps towards her, slow but firm, ominously unstoppable. The sound of his heels echoing on the stone, the way he held his head, the arrogant straightness of his long spine gave the movement a confident swagger that declared to everyone around that he was the one who was in control here—and he intended to stay that way.

'Do you know this man?' Rafe had found his voice.

'No!'

The panicked lie was stupid; she knew that as she saw the way that Guido's burning eyes narrowed sharply, the way that his head lifted even higher until it seemed that he was looking down his long, straight nose at her, pure contempt icing over his stunning features. And as it did, a sliver of that ice seemed to have formed at the nape of her neck, slithering its way down her trembling spine, chilling her skin as it went.

'Forgotten me already, *cara*?' he enquired with cruel silkiness. 'But then, I suppose that must be the case or I wouldn't find you here...'

That freezing gaze flicked from her ashen face to the altar, the waiting priest and back again.

'With him...'

This time the golden eyes acknowledged Rafe, standing at her side, but only for the briefest of seconds. Then they were fixed again on her face; holding her still in a way that made her feel like a butterfly pinned underneath a powerful microscope.

'Under these circumstances.'

To Amber's stunned bewilderment, a smile played over his sensual mouth. But it was a cruel smile, a torturer's smile. The smile that might appear on the face of a tiger just before it pounced to deliver the final death blow.

'Who the hell are you?'

Rafe's voice was belligerent and he made a move as if to take a step then obviously thought the better of it, stilling instead to remain at her side, the tension radiating from his long body.

The tiger's smile grew, became positively wicked.

'Allow me to introduce myself. My name is Guido Corsentino.'

Something in the name made Rafe take in a sharp breath. But he recovered almost immediately.

'And what have you to do with my wife?'

'Ah...but you see, she's really not your wife. Not yet.'

Guido actually appeared to look as if it mattered. He even let an expression that might have been regret drift across his face. But Amber knew that regret was the last thing on his mind. As was care for anyone else's feelings in this matter. He'd come here to create chaos and misery and was set on doing just that, not letting anyone get in his way.

'And I'm afraid she's not likely to be at any time in the near future.'

'And why is that?'

Amber's throat had closed so tight that she found it impossible to draw a breath with any ease. He couldn't do this to her—he just couldn't! Did he really hate her so much that he would hunt her down after all this time, just to destroy her one chance of happiness?

No! Please don't do this!

The words formed on her lips but she couldn't find the strength to give them any power and the thin thread of sound was absorbed by the concealing veil, no one even noticing that she had spoken. But her eyes locked with his, silently pleading with him, begging him to stop this now. To leave her alone and stop tormenting her. He'd had his fun—if that was what this cruel, sadistic game was to him—surely now he would go and leave them in peace?

He had to go. And it had to be a game. He hadn't wanted her in the past, when she would have lain down on the ground and let him walk all over her if it would have made him happy. But he'd made it plain that she meant nothing to him. So there was no reason at all why he should want her now. Except to cause trouble for her.

But it was painfully obvious that leaving was not what Guido had in mind.

'Why can't Amber ever become your wife?' he echoed the question sharply as if he simply couldn't understand why it had been asked.

The rich tones of his Italian accent had never sounded so strongly in Amber's ears, an accent that should have made his words sound soft and musical. Instead, it had exactly the opposite effect, making her freeze like some small, terrified animal facing an angry king cobra and just waiting for it to strike. She could only close her eyes and wait for the sting of his poison.

'Well, that is quite simple, really. She isn't in any position to be married—to anyone. You see, she already is married to me. That's right…' he added as he saw Rafe's disbelieving start, the way the other man's pale eyes went to the woman beside him, then back to his tormentor's dark, set face. 'Amber is married already. She happens to be *my* wife.'

CHAPTER TWO

IT HAD every bit of the effect he had wanted.

When he had thought about the moment when, after twelve long months of separation, he would finally confront the woman who had once been his wife—who was *still* his wife—he had known that he wanted it to really hit home to her. He had wanted her to be as stunned and shocked as he had been the day that she had walked out of his life to be with another man, leaving behind only a note that declared that she didn't love him any more.

That she had never loved him. Could never have loved a man like him.

That she had only married him in a moment of wild lunacy. An act she had regretted from the moment he had put the ring on her finger.

And now that he saw the type of man she really wanted to marry, he could understand why. The tall Englishman was exactly the sort of husband who would appeal to Amber Wellesley—Amber *Corsentino*'s—ingrained personal snobbery. With his pale skin, blond hair, blue eyes and narrow features, Rafe St Clair looked the sort of upper-class minor aristocrat who could give her the name and the status she had always craved. The name and the status that didn't come from marriage to a man who, together with his brother, had dragged himself up from the gutters of Siracusa, a man who didn't even know whose blood ran in his veins. It definitely wasn't the blue blood Amber had been looking for.

If he had thought that his very first words had created a silence, then it was like nothing when compared to the freezing stillness that had descended now. It was almost as if somehow the air inside the little church had frozen and no one dared move for fear of splintering it into a million irreparable shards. The only sound at all was the slight bang of the door as it fell shut behind the pregnant woman who had fainted and the two women who had helped her outside, probably cursing the fact that they were missing all the drama and the scandal.

'How can Amber be your wife?'

The crisp, clipped sound of Rafe St Clair's voice fitted perfectly too. That plum-in-the-mouth tone that always sounded as if the speaker was looking down his nose at the same time.

'In the same way that she planned to become yours—she married me.'

'That isn't true!'

It was Amber's voice that broke into his, her fearful tones echoing around the high roof of the church as she protested.

'I didn't…'

The Englishman looked down at the woman at his side, then back into Guido's face, and there was the flash of something inexplicable in his blue eyes.

'You're not married to him?'

He didn't seem to expect an answer, which was just as well, as Amber was clearly incapable of managing anything more. But he nodded and turned his attention back to the priest, who was standing uncertainly to one side, obviously not knowing how to react.

'The marriage will go ahead,' he instructed. 'Amber…'

'Do you want to be arrested for bigamy?' Guido flung the words at the bride, aiming them right at the huge, wide green eyes that were all he could see behind the concealing veil. Eyes that had once looked into his when she had declared that she loved him, that there was no other man in the world for her. 'Because that's what will happen if you go ahead. You cannot marry this man—you are married to me.'

'It wasn't legal!' It was a cry of despair as she saw her chance of marrying into the aristocracy disappear down the drain, Guido thought cynically. 'It wasn't even a real marriage!'

The silence that swelled around her words was shocking. It swirled and ebbed, like some terrible sea wave that threatened to take everything with it; swallow everything; drown everything.

Then:

'*Amber!*'

Even behind the veil, it was possible to see how Amber's face had lost every last trace of colour as her would-be groom turned shocked and stunned eyes on her, the tone of total disgust in which he said her name revealing how she had given herself away.

'I thought you said you didn't know this man but now… Is it true about this marriage?'

'And the rest?' This time the reproach came from a member of the congregation, a tall man whose narrow face and balding head made him an older version of the groom.

'Were you planning to trap my son into a *bigamous* marriage?' The revulsion in that word was plain; as was the black fury, the total rejection of her.

'I…'

Guido actually felt a twist of pity as he saw how she struggled for an answer; the way that her mouth opened and closed but no sound would come. But then her head went up, her green eyes flashed behind the lace and she fell back on the excuse she had given the first time.

'It wasn't a *real* marriage!'

Fiercely she directed a furious glare down the aisle at Guido. A glare so laser-hot that for a moment he almost believed it should have seared his skin, reduced that delicate veil to ashes as it burned through it.

'You have to believe me—you wouldn't think that I'd really marry someone like *him*?'

Every trace of that unexpected impulse to pity disappeared in a flash, shrivelled in the heat of her scorn, the blaze of her pride. And in its place was left an icy sense of loathing that blazed cold in his heart, turning pity to revulsion in the blink of an eye.

With deliberate slowness, his movements under the most rigid control, he reached into the inner pocket of his jacket and pulled out a folded sheet of white paper. He could feel the entire congregation watching, transfixed, held totally by what he was doing.

A flick of his hand shook open the folds, revealing an official form, a document bearing names and a date—his name—her name—and the date twelve months earlier on which they had been married.

'Looks real enough to me,' he drawled silkily, holding it up so that everyone could see.

'Let me…'

Rafe St Clair took a step forward, snatched the document from his hand, stared at it intently. His face was already pale with anger, but the way he compressed his mouth even more tightly etched further white lines around his nose and lips.

'Amber Christina Wellesley. Guido Ignazio Corsentino…'

His voice died, the paper crushed in his hand for a second before he flung it into Amber's face.

'You liar!'

'Rafe…'

But her protest was ignored.

'This wedding is cancelled,' Rafe declared. 'I wish you joy of your wife, Corsentino.'

'Rafe!' Amber tried again as he turned away. Unable to believe what was happening, the way that her life had been turned inside out, destroyed in the space of a few moments, she reached for his hand, wanting to stop him, make him stay. 'Rafe, *please*!'

But even before she had the chance to wrap her fingers around his, he was pulling away, flinging her from him as if he felt contaminated just by her touch. She had never seen his normally gentle-looking face harden into such antipathy. Her friend Rafe had disappeared and in his place was a total stranger.

'I want nothing to do with you! You disgust me—you little whore!'

'*No!*'

To Amber's astonishment, it was Guido who came to her defence, his voice harsh with fury, stepping forward, coming between her and the other man. She couldn't see what was on his face, in his eyes, but she saw Rafe's reaction to it, the way that he flinched, his head lowering, then backed away, moving hurriedly down the aisle. And as he went, his family got up too and followed him out.

The surprising kindness, protected by the last person on earth she might have expected to come to her aid, was the final straw. It took all her strength from her, weakened her legs so that they shook beneath her, unable to support her any longer.

With a low moan of despair she sank down on the steps of the altar and buried her face in her hands. Drained of all energy, she felt too flattened to think, too lost even to cry. She just retreated into the concealing, comforting darkness and hid there, letting her mind go blank until she found the courage to think again.

Vaguely she registered the sound of movements, the shuffle of bodies that she supposed must mean that the people in the congregation—the family and friends who had all come to see her married to Rafe—were now getting up and leaving. Footsteps made their way down the stone flagged aisle, the door creaked on its hinges, banged shut a few times, and then, slowly, gradually, every sound died away and she was left…

Alone?

Had everyone gone? Had every single person in the church walked out and left her here, by herself? Was she alone with her thoughts and nothing else?

Or was there someone there?

Was someone standing there in silence, not saying a word, just watching her? Seeing her in the depths of despair, struggling to cope with the way that her life had been shattered and now lay in tiny pieces around her feet?

Amber didn't really know which of the two prospects was worse. At this moment, she'd probably choose the latter because she didn't think she had the strength to cope with anyone. She knew that eventually she was going to have to look up, get up, and try very hard to pick up what little was left of her life. But right now, with her whole body trembling with the aftershocks from the emotional earthquake that had blasted through her, she just wanted a little while longer to stay here like this, to hide, to…

'Are you going to hide away like that for ever?'

The voice that broke into her protected world echoed her own thoughts so closely that for a moment she almost believed that she had asked the question of herself inside the privacy of her mind. But then reality registered in the fact that the tones in which the question had been asked were unmistakably masculine—and her heart twisted in shock at the realisation that they had also been shaded by a musical, sexy Italian accent.

Guido?

Was he still there? Was he the one who had stayed? Was it possible?

She would have expected that, having marched in here and set her world upside down, he had earned whatever satisfaction he had come for—the revenge he had wanted for the way she had walked out on him and their marriage.

The marriage that hadn't been a marriage.

The marriage that she had always believed hadn't been a marriage, but a farce, a deliberate ploy to use her, from start to finish. Which now Guido had openly declared before all these people...

'Well?'

It was harsher now, pushing at her, poking her mentally, driving her out of her cocoon, so that she dropped her concealing hand, flung her head up, turning on him with as much defiance as she could muster.

'I'm not hiding!'

'Looks like it to me,' Guido drawled mockingly. 'You have every appearance of a little girl hiding in a corner, away from something nasty—with an "if I do not see it then it isn't there and maybe if I am really lucky it will just go away" approach to life.'

'Well, if that's the case, then it's not working, is it?' Amber tossed at him, where he was lounging against the front of the very first pew, narrow hips resting on the polished wood, long legs stretched out at an angle. 'I've opened my eyes and the "something nasty" is very definitely still here.'

'And has no intention of going away either,' he finished for her, apparently unmoved by the furious insult that had just bounced off a skin that was thick as a rhinoceros hide.

He even smiled, though it was the smile of a killer snake. That dangerous king cobra was back, just waiting, just wanting her to tempt him to strike.

No—the description of a snake didn't fit Guido. The dark, lean, dangerous man who was lounging so indolently against the end of the pew was more like a lazily watchful hunting tiger, waiting for just the right moment to pounce.

Oh, dear...

Suddenly even her own thoughts struck Amber as ridiculous.

She was getting confused, getting her creatures muddled up. An impossible shudder of laughter bubbled up in her throat.

'Amber?'

Guido's voice sounded as if it came from a long, long way away. Had he moved? Was he leaving like all the others?

She should care more. After all, even her own mother had walked out on her, unable to bear the embarrassment of the way that the marriage had been brought to an abrupt halt; the embarrassment of finding that her daughter was already married.

'Amber, stop it!'

He'd definitely moved this time. His voice came from just above her and she could sense his presence in every cell in her body. Black-booted feet were set firmly on the stone flags just in front of her—she could see them through the strangely clinging veil—and the long black-clad columns of his legs, strong and muscular...

'Stop what? I just think it's so—funny!'

Her voice went up and down as if it were on a badly tuned radio, with the reception coming and going crazily.

'No, it's not!'

Hard hands clamped around her arms, hauling her to her feet—hauling her up against him so that her breath escaped her in a gasping rush.

'Yes, it is... Here I was—about to be married—and you turn up like...like three kinds of animal...'

'Three kinds of animal?' She'd confused him there. He was frowning down into her face, even his excellent English unable to cope with her fanciful imagination. 'Amber—stop crying and then we—'

Crying? What was he talking about? She wasn't crying; she was laughing.

'I'm not crying...'

She caught the sceptical look he turned on her, his bronze eyes even darker than usual.

'I'm *not!*'

'No?'

Releasing one arm, he touched the back of his free hand to

her neck and then slightly above that, to her chin, taking it away and looking hard at it before turning it so that she could see his bent knuckles.

They were wet, glistening with moisture that they had picked up from her skin. From the tears that she hadn't been aware of shedding and that were now, she realised, streaming silently down her cheeks and flowing onto her neck. That was why her veil felt as if it was crammed against her cheeks, almost glued to her skin.

Unnerved, she brushed at it with a trembling hand but only succeeded in pressing it even closer to her eyelashes.

'Let me…' Guido said but she was unable to stop herself from flinching back as he made to lift the fine lace.

'No…'

'*Dannazione*, Amber!' Guido swore. 'How can we talk when I can't even see your face with this thing in the way?'

'I don't want to talk—we have nothing to talk about! Today was the day I was supposed to be married to the man I wanted to wed—and you turn up and tell me I'm still married to you. To the man I most *don't* want to be married to in the world. To the man I never thought I was married to in the first place!'

'The man you *are* married to!'

It was only when she heard him confirm her fears that she finally realised she had to accept it. Even now, she admitted to herself, she had been holding on to a tiny, faint hope that this had all been a terrible mistake—a cruel, bitter game. She knew she had left Guido savagely angry, furious at the way she had walked out on him, and she frankly wasn't surprised that he wanted revenge for the insults she had tossed at him both verbally and in the letter she'd left behind.

Insults that had been her only hope of getting out of there and actually *leaving*. Making sure he never came after her; never called her back.

But this…

'The marriage *is* legal, then?'

'Do you doubt it?'

His tone spoke of arrogant disbelief of the fact that anyone should not believe him absolutely. And the way his broad shoulders stiffened, the long spine straightening and his proud head coming up, only reinforced the message of controlled fury in his voice.

'Do you think I would go to this trouble for a marriage that wasn't real?'

'But you said…'

It sure as hell isn't a real marriage! he'd said. *There's been nothing real about it from the start.*

'I know what I said, Amber, but…*porca miseria*!' Guido swore in exasperation so violent that his explosive words echoed around the now empty church. 'I cannot speak to you like this!'

Coming close again, but soft-footed this time, he hooked his hands under the fall of the veil, taking it between his finger and thumb at either side.

'Allow me…'

Amber wished she could stop him but she seemed to have lost all strength to act. Her feet were rooted to the ground and she couldn't force them to move. It was as if the gentleness in his voice had drained all the power from her so that she could only stand there in silence and wait.

'At least if we can see each other, Amber, *mia bella*,' Guido murmured, 'then maybe we can talk…'

She wasn't his beautiful one, Amber thought frantically; she didn't want to be *anything* to him! And why, now, when she was little prepared for it, when it was the last thing she wanted, did he have to say her name in that very special way that he had, with the last R rolled out on his tongue, sounding almost like a deep, deep purr? A tiger's purr.

Just for a second hysteria threatened again. Her lips trembled, her mind shaking…

And then Guido lifted the veil and their eyes met and suddenly every last thought of laughter, or fight—or anything—went right out of her like air out of a pricked balloon, leaving her limp and lost and unable to think.

Unable to think beyond...

'Guido...'

Beyond the fact that she remembered those eyes looking down into hers. She remembered the scent of his skin, the touch of his hands. She remembered how it had felt to have that devastatingly sensual mouth on hers, to taste his lips, feel the caressing sweep of his tongue. She remembered it—and she wanted it all over again.

She wanted it so much that she could almost taste it. That when she let her own tongue slide across her parched mouth, she could almost believe that there would be the taste of him lingering there. Even after all this time.

'Amber...'

And she knew that tone too. Knew the thickness in his voice that meant he had been caught on the raw by the sudden rush of sensuality. The one that had her in its grip too—drying her mouth and changing her eyes as it darkened his, turning them from burning bronze to the blackness of passion. She watched the heavy lids slide half-closed in a way that gave him a slumberous, barely awake look in a way that she knew from experience was deeply deceptive.

When he looked like that, then he was far from sleep. In fact he was at his most vividly awake, most fiercely aroused. His blood was heating with passion, his body waking to need, and if she stood any closer then she would feel the hard, proud force of that hunger pressed against her in evidence of the way he was feeling.

Guido made a rough, raw sound in the back of his throat, and snatched in a breath as if he could hardly make his lungs work to keep himself alive.

'I have to…' he said huskily and she could hear the fight he was having with himself in the jagged edge to the words, the way his voice sounded hoarse as if it hadn't been used for days.

She knew the moment too that he lost the fight. It was there in the momentary way that he closed his eyes, the breath that hissed through his teeth, before, in a moment that was part conquest, part defeat, he lowered his dark head and took her mouth with his.

CHAPTER THREE

IDIOTA! Idiota!

The reproach to himself was a refrain over and over inside Guido's head.

Corsentino, you are a fool!

He shouldn't be doing this—it was the last thing on earth that he should be doing! But he couldn't stop himself.

From the moment that he had lifted the veil and seen Amber's face, green eyes looking up into his, breathed in the scent of her skin, warm and soft, and vanilla and spice, he had known what was going to happen. His gaze had fixed on her mouth, softly sensual, partly open, and he could remember so vividly how it had tasted, how it had felt under his.

And he wanted to experience that again.

So he gave up the fight to stop himself. Gave in to the impulse that pushed him. Gave himself up to the need that was nagging at him.

'Amber…'

The sound of her name was a breath between their lips, a moment before they met, before he felt…

A year was a long time. Too long without the taste, the feel, the scent of the woman whose body had once driven him out of his mind with lust.

Once?

Guido's breath caught in his throat as he almost let the disbelieving laughter escape.

Once, be damned. He had known from the minute he had set eyes on her again—set eyes only on her back, for God's sake!—that he was lost. Lost again. Caught up in the coils of the hunger that had bound him to her the first time. Burned in the heat of the need she could create just by existing. Drawn by the silent, instinctive signals that her body somehow sent out to his.

That was why he had stayed when everyone else had walked out.

Even her mother had walked out—sweeping past him with her nose in the air and an expression that said he was less than the dirt beneath her feet.

But at least she had looked at him. She hadn't even spared her daughter a second glance.

She hadn't looked at Amber, sitting there in a crumpled heap on the altar steps. She hadn't shown a hint of care or compassion or—anything! She had just walked straight out of the church, following the groom's mother and father as if they were all that mattered. As if they and not her daughter were her real family.

It had only taken a few moments and then they were alone together, with Amber still curled into a miserable little ball on the marble steps to the altar.

Guido had tried to turn. He had wanted to go—he'd done what he came for, stopped the bigamous and illegal wedding, had the revenge he needed for the way she had treated him, the callous way she had walked out on him when she'd decided that he wasn't good enough for her. He'd even avenged the way that Rafe St Clair had treated one of his own family not too long before. It was what he'd planned—walk in—blow the proceedings and her hope of an aristocratic marriage to hell—and walk out again.

But his conscience wouldn't let him.

His conscience and something deeper, harder, more primitive. Something that kicked him hard in the gut—and lower—when he tried to turn round and leave.

Something that had nothing to do with sympathy and caring and everything to do with hunger and need and the eternal, endless fires that burned between men and women from the start of the world until the end of time. And had flamed between him and this woman from the very first moment in which they'd met.

He simply couldn't walk out on her as she had done to him and that was an end to it.

And he couldn't walk out without touching her, tasting her—taking her mouth just one more time.

And so he ignored all the warnings that his brain threw at him, listened instead to the most primitive, most male parts of himself, and bent his head and kissed her.

'Ahh, Amber...'

The scent of her body surrounded him, flooding his head. Those warm pink lips, previously clamped tight to hold back bitter and violent emotions, seemed to tense even further for a second then, slowly, painfully slowly, gave, softened...opened...

His throat clenched, his heart jerking. His body hardened. And the thoughts that filled his mind were definitely inappropriate, positively sinful, given the place where he stood, in the centre of those altar steps.

She was warm and soft against him. Melting pliantly into the hardness of his body. And if he thought that he had known sexual hunger before, that he had desired her in the past, then it was as nothing when compared to the burning hands that took his nerves now and held them tight—twisted them hard.

'Mia cara,' he muttered, raw and thick, his hands sliding down from where he had held her arms as he hauled her to her feet. Moving over her back, down the fine line of her spine to the narrow waist.

'Mia bella...'

He wanted to press her closer, to hold her tight, to feel the delicacy of her slender frame against him, but at the same time wanted his hands to be everywhere. Stroking over the fine silk of her dress, feeling the curves and lines of what lay beneath; closing over the softness of female flesh on her exposed arms; smoothing and cupping the swell of her hips, the neat buttocks.

'Bella...'

It was a groan of need on his mouth. But even as it escaped him he knew that he didn't want to talk. That he only wanted to feel, to taste, to enjoy.

Her small pink tongue tangled with his, in much the same way that his restless fingers tangled with a wayward curl of chestnut hair that he had tugged loose at the nape of her neck. The sensual slide of his fingertips against the silky strands, the intimate taste of her warm, moist mouth made him gasp out loud in the same moment that Amber sighed his name, taking the faint sound into her throat and swallowing it down with a moan that drove his already heated senses wild.

She swayed against him, arms hanging limp by her sides, the delicate flowers in her bouquet brushing against his leg, crushing their petals and releasing the odour into the air to float upwards towards his nose. With his senses already inflamed, this new sensation threatened overload, setting up a pounding at his temples that destroyed any attempt at rational thought. His hungry hands clutched rather than stroked, sought the swell of her breasts, warm beneath the silk, soft, yielding...

'Bellissima—mia moglie...'

'No!'

That last word had been a mistake. Her spine had stiffened, her tongue stilling, her head pulling just an inch back. So short a distance and yet one that put all the division in the world between them. Because of course Amber knew just enough Italian to understand those two emotive, provoking words, 'mia moglie'—my wife.

'No, no, no, no!'

With a brutal effort Amber wrenched her mouth away from his lips, wrenched her body from his constraining hands. Wrenched her mind back from the terrible, dangerous cliff edge over which she had almost, foolishly, crazily tumbled.

'No! I am not your wife!'

'Oh, but you are.'

It was low, fast, deadly as a striking snake, and every bit as lethal to her self-control.

'But I don't want to be married to you!'

'Then you should have thought of that before you said "I do" twelve months ago.'

'This has to be a bad dream!' she managed, shaking her head in despair.' The worst possible nightmare...'

'Believe that if you wish, *mia cara*, but I assure you that you are wide awake and nothing can make this anything but real. Do you think I would go to all this trouble if it wasn't?'

You're just not worth it, his tone implied. He wouldn't have expended the time and effort to travel all the way from the heat of Sicily to the cool springtime of this little Yorkshire village, if he hadn't been forced to do so by circumstances beyond his control.

'And really you should be grateful to me.'

'Grateful?'

Amber knew that she was gaping, that her jaw had dropped and her mouth was almost as wide open as her eyes. But she just couldn't believe what she was hearing.

'And why, in God's name, should I be grateful to you for what you've done?' she asked in a voice that was so rigid with shock and distress it actually sounded as coldly distant as she might have wanted had she had the strength of mind to control it properly.

'Didn't I just save you from prison?' Guido drawled with indolent arrogance. 'So tell me—what is the sentence for bigamy here in England? Five years? Ten?'

'This—our marriage truly was real?'

She still couldn't get her head round the appalling facts even though Guido had hammered them home several times since his dramatic arrival in the church.

'It's absolutely real—totally legal, watertight and binding. We're husband and wife whether we like it or not.'

'Not.'

It was all she could manage. How could she be happy to learn that the marriage she believed was just a con, a ploy to keep her right where Guido had wanted her—in his bed—was actually the genuine thing, and still binding after all this time?

A year ago, she would have been overjoyed to think that she had been wrong and the marriage she'd thought was a sham was in fact the genuine thing, but then she had been naïve as a baby and so desperately in love with this man that she would have lain down on the ground and let him walk all over her if that was what he wanted.

Now the thought of being tied to him, legally, emotionally, in any way, was like an appalling life sentence, a unendurable term handed down by the cruellest of judges—the fates who had her future in their hands.

'I don't want this!'

'And neither do I,' Guido assured her darkly. 'But right now it seems that we have no choice. We're married—linked together for better or for worse and we have to accept that. The only thing we can consider is what we are going to do about it.'

That 'we' unmanned her. It took her breath away; made her legs tremble. She had thought that she was going to have to face this all on her own—that he had destroyed everything she believed, had taken everything away and now…

The only thing we can consider is what we are going to do about it.

But she didn't want it to be 'we'—because that meant a connection with him and she didn't want to be with him for any reason whatsoever.

'We aren't going to do anything!' she declared, somehow finding the strength to bring her chin up high, green eyes blazing as she faced him out. 'I don't want anything to do with you and I certainly don't want you interfering in my life ever again.'

'You left me no choice,' Guido pointed out with a coolly controlled reasonableness that chilled her blood just to hear it. 'Someone had to stop you from making the worst mistake of your life.'

'Oh, no, this wasn't the worst mistake I've ever made.'

Amber shook her head so violently that another set of strands of hair escaped from their elaborate pinning and fell loose around her face.

'That was when I married you—and unfortunately for me, there was no one around to stop me making such a terrible mistake as I did then. This is small potatoes compared with that.'

If only she could believe that. It would help if she could convince herself, because then she might be able to deliver the words in a tone that would also convince this dark, hard-faced monster standing before her with his arms folded tight across his powerful chest, his heavy-lidded eyes scrutinising her face intently, watching every play of emotion as they came and went across her features.

'You've ruined my life, destroyed my hopes of a future and I most definitely do not want you staying around, making things even worse, and forcing me to endure your hateful presence as an added form of torture. I'll handle this myself!'

Gathering up the long silken skirts of her dress—her wedding dress, she reminded herself on a choke of bitter distress—she whirled away from him and set off, marching away from the altar and down the aisle, the sound of her heels on the stone flags seeming appallingly loud in the silence.

'And what do you think you can do?'

He flung the challenge after her with such force that she almost believed she could feel it hitting against the back she had turned on him, running down her spine in a cold, brutal shiver. But she refused to let it, or the scepticism in his tone deter her in the least.

'I'll think of something!' she tossed over her shoulder at him, forcing herself to keep moving, to not let the sudden weakness in her legs slow her or hold her back. 'I'll do anything— anything at all.'

'Even face the divorce courts?'

'That will be the first place I'll be heading as soon as I get out of here.'

'And the papers?'

'Papers?'

In spite of herself she couldn't control the sudden tremble of nerves that threatened to make her miss her footing, slowed her furious stride, made it wobble a bit from side to side.

'What would the papers want with this?'

Try as she might, she couldn't force herself to go on, stumbling to an abrupt halt before her legs gave way altogether. She had to struggle to make it look as if she had just turned in genuine curiosity, half-leaning against the end of a nearby pew, but keeping her face turned towards the door as much as she could.

'I can see the headlines now—"*Society wedding ends in chaos…*"'

Guido's voice floated down the aisle towards her, the dark vein of mockery making her wince inwardly and clench her teeth tight against the whimper of protest that almost escaped.

'"*Baronet's son jilted at the altar by deceitful fiancée.*"'

'I didn't…' Amber began protestingly but Guido ignored her and carried on with his cold-hearted litany, his tone growing harsher, darker, more brutally triumphant with each word.

'"*Bigamous bride outed as she prepares to lie her way into a title and a fortune.*"'

'I wasn't lying! I didn't know!'

'You're not denying the title and the fortune part, I see.' The statement stabbed like a stiletto between her ribs.

'I'm not denying anything—or confirming anything, for that matter.'

Somehow Amber found new strength to make herself move again, putting one foot in front of the other to get herself to the end of the aisle, reach a point where she could put her hand on the door.

'I'm not even going to talk to you about this any more!'

She had to get out of here! Get away from him and his cruelty and accusations. Away from the tidal waves of bitter memories that swamped her each time she so much as looked at him. Just seeing him had been bad enough—but that kiss…!

Just what had she been thinking of to let him kiss her like that—to respond as she had? Had she no strength, no pride—no…?

All thought died away in a rush as she pulled the heavy door open and, blinking for a moment in the sunlight, saw just what was waiting for her outside.

Or, rather, saw just who was waiting for her.

The small crowd of people who had gathered to watch her arrive for the wedding had grown. There was now what looked like a sea of people milling around at the lych-gate and as soon as they saw her appear in the doorway they started to rush forward.

'Miss Wellesley! Just a word…'

Something flashed, hard and bright, making her blink desperately, eyes suddenly watering in shock. Another flash followed—and another—so that she put up her hand to shield her face.

'Is it true that you're already married, Miss Wellesley—to Guido Corsentino?'

'Did you really think you could get away with bigamy?'

'Just how many husbands do you have, Amber?'

Amber reeled back as microphones were pushed at her, almost into her face. The crowd had surged forward, hemming her in, and they were not, she saw now, the friendly, smiling villagers she had waved to on her way into the church. Some had microphones, others notebooks, and everywhere, on all sides, were those flashes that she now saw came from cameras. Cameras that were pointed directly at her and clicking furiously.

'I…' she began, but both her mind and her voice failed her in the same minute. Panic clutched at her throat so she couldn't force any sound from it and the same fear fused her thought processes so that she couldn't have found a thing to say anyway.

'I…' she tried again, only to break off on a squeal of fear as the crowd surged forward, threatening to engulf her.

Her frantic step backwards made the narrow heel of her shoe catch in the hem of her long silk skirt, throwing her off balance, and she would have fallen but for the strength of a hard male arm that came round her, clamping tight about her waist and holding her upright. Another hand reached for the door, pushing it forward so that it formed a barrier against the pushing, shouting mob.

'No comment!' a cold, harshly accented voice declared. 'Not now. You'll get your story later!'

And the forceful statement was further emphasised by the slamming of the door tight shut right in the face of the most forward photographer. Not troubling to release her, Guido slammed the bolt home on the door and leaned back against it, taking her with him in his imprisoning embrace.

'I did warn you!' he declared, burning bronze eyes blazing down into hers. 'News obviously travels fast around here.'

'But—how…'

Even as she stammered out the words, Amber knew the answer to the question.

There had already been a lot of newspaper interest in her wedding to Rafe. The marriage of the heir to one of the largest estates in the country, along with an earldom that brought him to one of the highest ranks of the aristocracy, was bound to be news. Add into that the fact that for a long time Rafe had been the subject of stories in the tabloids and magazines, his slender blond looks stirring interest and speculation, and you had the perfect subject for the gossip columns.

Their engagement had created a buzz of interest, their marriage preparations had had the spotlight of attention focused on them.

And now, of course, the debacle of the wedding, the failure of that marriage before it had begun—and the appalling accusation of possible bigamy—had turned a spark of interest into a blazing inferno of gossip in the space of less than an hour.

'What am I going to do?'

The question wasn't addressed to Guido, but rather to the malign fate that had brought him back into her life at this particular moment. She still couldn't believe that it had happened—couldn't begin to think how it had happened.

She had been so sure that her short, rash and desperately ill-fated marriage to Guido Corsentino had been a fake. He had told her that it wasn't valid. That their wild, whirlwind romance had just been a fantasy of her imagination; their even more crazy rush to the altar in a Las Vegas chapel only a pragmatic act on his part in order to get what he wanted.

'It sure as hell wasn't a proper marriage.' The sound of the cruel words he had flung at her was so clear inside her head that for a moment she almost thought that he had spoken them out loud here once again. *'It was a farce from start to finish. But it worked didn't it? It kept you in my bed, which was what it was intended to do.'*

At the time she had thought that that was all the marriage had done. That it had all been a pretence. But now it seemed that she was legally bound to this man and as a result all her hopes for her life, for her future, lay in ruins.

Through the haze that blurred her eyes, part desperation, part tears, Amber struggled to look up into the face of the man who held her, needing—longing—to know just what was in his mind.

What had he meant when he'd said "The only thing we can consider is what we are going to do about it"?

What did he plan for her and her future? And what was his next move going to be? Just the thought of it made her shiver as if she had found herself hiding, cowering in the jungle, frozen with fear, just waiting for the prowling tiger to pounce.

'You said—you said they'd get their story later,' she managed, forcing the words past lips that suddenly seemed wooden and stiff with fright.

'And so they will,' Guido returned with stunning calm. 'Just as soon as we come up with the story we want them to believe.'

There it was again, that 'we' that took everything out of her hands and put Guido right in control whether she wanted it or not.

And the truth was that right now she had no idea at all what she wanted—or how she was going to go about getting it. Held close to him like this, she was painfully aware of the burning heat of Guido's body next to hers, of the steel-hard band of his arm clamped tight around her waist, crushing her close and constricting her breathing

'We?'

He might feel hot, Amber realised, but his brain was very definitely cool. Definitely in controlled, analytical mode. Even the swollen arousal she had felt in his body before had now eased and she could almost hear the calm ticking-over of his brain as he assessed the situation, considered his options and came up with a plan.

'Why we…?'

Dark eyes looked down into hers, cold and assessing and totally in control.

'Because we have no other option,' he stated calmly. 'The Press have seen us together—your family—your fiancé's family have too. From now on we're in this together, whether we like it or not.'

CHAPTER FOUR

FROM now on we're in this together, whether we like it or not.

And Amber didn't like it; not one little bit. It was obvious—Guido could see it in her face. In the way that her eyes shadowed, the tension that pulled her pretty jaw tight, clamped her soft lips together. She wanted out of this—and she wanted him out of her life, that much was plain. But right now he really didn't see that they had any sort of a choice.

'And just what sort of a story did you have in mind?'

Her voice was cold and clipped, her tone matching the frost in her gaze, the way that those beautiful green eyes flicked over him, looking him up and down with cool contempt.

Something that she was going to like even less than the thought of them working together. And it was the obvious distaste on her face that made him all the more determined to carry it through.

The idea had come to him when he'd seen her gathering up her skirts and heading down the aisle away from him. Running away from him as fast as she had done that first time—and the burn of rejection had been as bitter and as savage as ever.

He had known in that moment that he couldn't let her go.

Just moments before he had held her in his arms and kissed her and his body had throbbed with the heated, hungry passion that he had believed was dead to him—long dead. Certainly no

woman had stirred that same hot yearning in twelve empty
months as this Amber Wellesley—Amber *Corsentino*—seemed
to be able to create in the space of a single heartbeat.

He'd seen her and his body had started to crave everything
this woman had once brought him. He'd touched her and that
craving had grown into an uncontrollable desire. He'd kissed
her and every sense had gone up in flames, unable to bear the
torment of being separate from her.

But Guido had to content himself with that kiss. Knowing
all the time that he was only stirring up trouble for himself.
Stirring up the memories, the needs, the passion that he had
thought was long since buried, tamped down hard, hidden under
the hard, bitter weight of the feelings she had left him with on
the day she had walked out of his life.

Feelings he had spent the past year trying to forget—trying
and failing miserably.

And so when he had seen her running away from him once
more, he had known, deep in his soul, that he couldn't let it
happen again. He couldn't let this woman walk out of his life
without having her once more.

'No!'

The only way he could get a grip on his thoughts was to say
the word out loud, making Amber blink in shock as she stared
at him, green eyes shadowed with confusion.

'No?' she questioned shakily. 'No, you have no story to tell
them? Or no—?'

'Oh, I've a story we can give them, all right …'

Suddenly horrifyingly aware of the fact that he still held her
close, Guido released Amber with an abruptness that almost
dropped her to the ground, making her stagger back in shocked
bewilderment, her hand going out to the wall to steady herself.

'Then tell me!'

'You're not…' Guido began, then caught himself up sharply.
What was the point of warning her, letting her prepare

herself? She was going to fight him on this, anyway. He could see it in her face. She'd fight him all the way, no matter what she said. So he might as well just let her have it straight and take it from there. At least that way he'd have the advantage of surprise once more, as he had when he'd arrived at the church.

The memory of the way she'd frozen when he'd spoken, the time it had taken her to turn round, was still clear in his memory. He'd been planning that moment for weeks, ever since he'd learned of her upcoming marriage, and it had brought a dark satisfaction to his soul. The sort of satisfaction he wanted to know again.

'Let them think we're a couple.'

'What?'

There was no need to ask what she thought of his suggestion. It was etched into her lovely face, darkening the pools of her eyes above cheeks that had gone white in appalled shock.

'Let them…?'

'Let them think we're back together.'

'You have to be joking!'

'No joke.' Guido shook his dark head emphatically. 'It's the only way you're going to walk out of here with any sort of reputation—and able to look people in the eye. Your chances of marriage to St Clair are ruined…'

'Thanks to you!'

Guido glanced down at the tight little fists into which she had clenched her hands. He could read in her eyes the way she was tempted to launch herself at him, raise her fist to pound him on the shoulder, maybe even hit him in the face.

Perhaps he should tell her the truth about her supposed bridegroom. If she knew the real Rafe St Clair and the way that the man had been prepared to use her for his own ends, then would she be so quick to attack? Would she fight so hard for him then?

'You've destroyed my life!'

'No, *cara*,' Guido reproved silkily. 'You did that for yourself

when you tried to get yourself a new groom without making
sure that you had got rid of the old one first.'

'You said it was not a legal marriage!'

'I said we didn't have any sort of real marriage—it's not at
all the same thing. The marriage you walked out on was perfectly legal, perfectly binding, as you would have found out if
you had bothered checking.'

'It didn't seem necessary.'

Amber couldn't believe she had been such a fool. Ever since
the day that she had walked out on Guido, she had struggled to
put their charade of a marriage behind her. It had been bad
enough thinking that Guido had only gone through the
ceremony to control her, to keep her in his bed. To find that she
had swallowed the idea of it being real when in fact it had just
been a fake, set up to deceive her, had twisted the original knife
in even deeper.

As a result, she had ruthlessly locked away all thoughts of
that day into a sealed compartment in her memory, refusing to
let herself bring them out to look at them for any reasons whatsoever. When Rafe had asked her to marry him, she had
wondered briefly if she should check on the legality of her first
'wedding'. But the memory of Guido's brutal tone, his cal-
lously scornful words, had made her flinch right away from
even thinking about it.

Fear had added an extra impetus too, she admitted, feeling
the sense of horror that had gripped her then take her by the
throat once again. If she had found that the Las Vegas ceremony
had been binding, then she would have had to admit it to Rafe,
and—far worse—she would have had to connect with Guido
in order to arrange for a divorce.

Cravenly—and foolishly, it now seemed—she had dodged
away from the whole issue and had let herself believe that
there had been no earlier marriage to stand in the way of the
present one.

'To tell you the truth, I didn't even remember our time together,' she lied in a desperate attempt to protect herself from the anguish that was slashing at her heart. 'It didn't really matter.'

She'd got in a knife cut of her own that time, she saw as she watched the flames of dark anger blaze in the depths of his eyes. His jaw clamped tight shut over the flare of anger and a muscle tugged in his cheek.

Hastily she backed away, down the aisle, moving into one of the pews so as to put the strength of the wood between him and her. She felt better that way. He'd never, ever hurt her physically but the emotional anguish he'd put her through had been hard enough to bear. Not that any wood, however strong and solid, was any sort of protection against a broken heart.

'So you were in such a rush to become a lady that you didn't care whether this marriage was lawful or not also?' Guido questioned stiffly. 'You really should not be so careless about the legalities of your weddings, *carissima*. Now you've lost the title you aimed for...'

'And the husband I wanted!'

That brought him up sharp. For a moment something new flared in those deep-set eyes. Something that wasn't anger but something darker and more dangerous even than his fury had been.

'So I'm supposed to believe that the man himself was what you really wanted in all this? You aren't going to claim that you loved him, are you?'

Amber's hands folded over the edge of the pew back, holding on tight until her knuckles showed white under her stretched skin. She knew she was on very dangerous ground here. One false step and she could give herself away completely, putting herself right into her tormentor's hands and giving him the perfect set of weapons to torture her with.

'Did you even consider that before you marched in here and broke up my life?' she demanded, her harsh, tight voice echoing around the high, arching roof of the church. 'Did it make you pause to think about what you were doing?'

'Why does that matter?' Guido countered harshly. 'Did you love him?'

Oh, how she wished she could say that yes, she loved Rafe. That she adored him. She longed to be able to fling her defiance right into his face but even as she opened her mouth the need for honesty caught her on the raw.

She hadn't been marrying for love, she'd known that right from the start. But she had tried love once and it had blown up right in her face. She didn't dare to risk that sort of bitter disillusionment all over again. So she was marrying for friendship—warm, gentle friendship. Without the savage bite of passion that had taken her heart and shattered it into a million irreparable pieces. She was marrying for freedom, for comfort and—yes—finally, for once in her life, to make her mother smile.

And Pamela Wellesley had smiled, at least for a moment or two. She had smiled when the engagement was announced. And she had smiled today when they had set out for the church and this wedding that meant so much to her.

'I wanted to marry him,' she managed stiltedly.

'Oh, I'll just bet you did. After all, the Honourable Rafe St Clair had so much more to offer you than an apparently penniless photographer trying to earn a living in Las Vegas.'

'Apparently?'

She'd caught the unexpected word and looked up, turning a puzzled face in his direction. But Guido offered no hint of explanation. Instead he lifted one hand in an arrogantly dismissive gesture, brushing aside her question as if it were a buzzing fly that annoyed him.

'But this won't solve our immediate problem. The paparazzi outside won't wait for ever. They want a story and the sooner the better. We should give them one—'

'The one we should give them being that we are still a

couple,' Amber interjected, the cynicism and disbelief in her intonation making it plain just what she thought of that.

'That we are back together again,' Guido corrected smoothly. 'They'll love that!'

'They might, but I most definitely won't. And I can't think why you should even imagine that it would work.'

'Your English Press adore a love story—they want to write about that perfect ending where two people live happily after all.'

'Happily ever after,' Amber corrected automatically, the unwanted thought—*if only it could be true*—slicing at her from deep inside. 'And you know only too well that I didn't mean it wouldn't work for them—but that there's no way it would work for me!'

'It doesn't have to work for you,' Guido dismissed scornfully. 'It only has to work for the Press. And if we convince them that you were not thinking clearly when you agreed to marry Rafe, because you were broken-hearted…'

'At losing you?' Amber scoffed, needing to put the scorn into her voice to hide the way that unease twisted her nerves so painfully. Guido's fictional scenario was coming way too close to the truth for comfort. 'Tell me about it!'

'But now that we've met up again—no matter under what circumstances…' Guido persisted, blatantly ignoring her cynical interjection. 'We…'

'Don't tell me—we looked into each other's eyes and realised that we still cared so desperately for each other that we fell into each other's arms…'

That was something she could dismiss without hesitation. At least she thought she could, so it was doubly disconcerting to feel those already twisted nerves tighten even more painfully as she spoke.

'Something like that. It does not matter how we word it. Anything, so long as we go out of this church together to face that rat pack out there and give them a story with a positive spin on it that they can print in tomorrow's editions.'

'And you really believe they'll run with it?'

She had to admit that she was tempted. For all sorts of reasons.

When her world had come crashing down with Guido's explosive arrival at the aborted wedding ceremony—was it really barely half an hour ago?—she hadn't been able to think beyond the immediate moment. All she had wanted then was to be left alone and to find a hole—the tinier the better—into which she could crawl to hide herself. Somewhere that she could lick her wounds, wait for the world to stop spinning in the sickening way it had been doing ever since that horrific interruption, and pray that one day things would quieten down so that she could dare to venture out again.

But that wasn't going to happen. There wasn't anywhere she could go; no one she could turn to.

Except Guido.

She had burned her boats with Rafe, that much was obvious. The sheer hatred in his eyes when he had turned to her, the venom with which he had spat the brutal insult at her, had made that only too plain. And who could blame him?

With Rafe had gone all his family, of course. The St Clairs were never likely to forgive the insult to their family honour that they believed she had inflicted today. What were they to expect from the Wellesley family? they would be saying. Like mother like daughter, after all. They'd always known it.

Her mother, too, would never forgive her for the public humiliation. That would be just one more thing to add to the long list of faults for which she could never atone, this one being the last and the worst in Pamela's eyes. It would leave a stain that could never be erased. So there was no hope of help there, or comfort, or support.

There was no one in the world she could turn to.

Except Guido.

For the first time in the long-drawn-out minutes since she had taken refuge in the narrow wooden pew, Amber made herself look straight at Guido. She saw the way that the long, powerful body was leaning back against the heavy oak church door, behind which she could still vaguely hear the murmur of voices from the crowd. Every now and then someone would rap hard on that door, destroying her hope that the reporters and photographers might have given up in boredom and gone home.

Even as the thought entered her mind, another of those loud, aggressive knocks came from outside, making her flinch inside at the sound. And this time it was accompanied by an even louder voice calling her name, and asking for, 'Just a word, Miss Wellesley—a few questions! You have to come out of there some time!'

Fearfully Amber let her eyes fly to Guido's face, seeing there nothing of her own nervous apprehension. Instead, he seemed totally relaxed, his proud head flung back so that it rested on the edge of the door, muscular arms folded over the width of his chest. Long legs crossed at the ankles were stretched taut, pulling the fine material of his trousers tight against narrow hips and muscular thighs in a way that made her mouth dry in basic, sensual response.

His face too was totally calm, the strong jaw relaxed, the dark eyes only slightly hooded as he met her assessing stare with cool composure. He was between her and the 'enemy' outside—and so he seemed like a protector—but were appearances deceiving her? Was Guido the only real enemy?

She couldn't begin to guess at the answer, only knowing that right now, in the situation in which she found herself, he seemed like her only possible hope.

'Put it this way,' Guido said at last. 'I think that this is the only way for you to walk out of here on any sort of a positive note. You can leave this church with me—as my wife—or you can take your chance with the vultures outside.'

'I think that's what they call being caught between a rock and a hard place.'

Amber tried for an airy laugh and failed miserably, succeeding only in sounding cold and cynical even to her own ears. And it earned her another of those dark, glowering frowns, anger flashing in the deep-set eyes.

'Then I am to take it that that is a no?' he questioned harshly, levering himself away from the door so that he stood upright.

Amber knew it was impossible that he could have grown even half an inch taller in the time that he had been leaning back like that, but even so she had the irrational feeling that he had done just that. Grown bigger and stronger, his shoulders broadening, his head held higher so that he was even more imposing than he had ever been before.

The thought took all the strength from her legs so that she sank back onto the worn wooden seat of the pew, her hand twisting in the fine white silk of her dress. Her wedding dress. For a moment there she had almost forgotten.

'Well?' Guido prompted curtly when the thought dried her mouth too so that she couldn't find any sort of an answer to give him.

'I...'

Twice Amber opened her mouth to respond and both times her voice failed her completely, fading to a weak croak after the single word. How could she answer? What could she possibly say? It seemed that no matter which way she turned, something terrible and unbearable waited for her. So how did she choose the lesser of all those evils?

'Così sia!'

Guido flung out his hands in a very Italian gesture, dismissing the whole topic and seeming to fling it from him.

'If that's the way you want it, then so be it! You can handle this alone.'

He had turned and headed back to the church door before

she quite realised what he was doing. That he was leaving—that he had every intention of just walking out and leaving her here. Alone. And of course when he opened the door then the reporters and cameramen would just pour in...

Panic pushed her to her feet again, holding fast to the end of the pew as she took a couple of frantic steps into the aisle.

'Wait!'

He actually had his fingers on the big metal door handle, was about to turn it... For the space of half a dozen uneven, fearful heartbeats, she thought that he hadn't heard or, if he had, then he was determined to ignore her desperate cry. But then, very slowly, Guido stopped. His hand stilled on the big metal ring, then loosened, dropping down to his side again. He spared her just the smallest flick of a glance over his shoulder in her direction. That was all.

'Wait?' he said at last. 'For what?'

'For—for my answer.' Amber stumbled over the words in her haste to get them out. Seeing him prepared to walk away like that had focused her mind brutally, She had no doubt at all now what she wanted; which way she had to go. There was only one way she could go.

'And that answer is?'

Still he kept turned away from her and she wished he would turn round. It was so hard to speak to the long, straight back, to see nothing of his face but just the sleek, shining mane of black hair.

'My answer is—you know what it is—it's— Oh, please, won't you just turn round?'

'As you wish...'

He took his time about it, turning so slowly that she had time to rethink her request not once but twice while he did so. And when he was at last facing her again, those polished bronze eyes fixed on her face, she had to swallow hard to relieve the agonising tension in her throat. Now she wished she'd kept her mouth shut and let him stay where he was. Surely saying what she had to say to the back of his head couldn't have been as bad, as nerve-racking as doing it now, to his face. Where all his features seemed to be carved from stone, and those eyes were as cold and hard as ice.

He didn't speak again but just waited—and watched the play of emotions over her face as she struggled for the strength to speak again. And he wouldn't say anything until she did, that much was obvious.

But still, could she come right out and say it? Say 'Yes, I'll do it. I'll leave here with you—on your arm—as your wife— making public what for the past year has been my shameful little secret, the one I always prayed that no one would ever find out?'

And so she hedged, moving on to another topic. One that was almost as difficult—but one she sincerely needed an answer to.

'There—there's one thing I need to know.'

Guido kept silent when she paused, only the faint lift of his head, the way he tilted it to one side, revealing the fact that he had heard her and was waiting for her to elaborate.

'I don't really understand. If we do this—'

When we do this, because what choice did she have?

'Then what would you get out of it?'

Guido didn't hesitate and his deep, dark gaze didn't waver for a second but remained so fixed on hers that she felt it might have the effect of a searing laser, marking her permanently like a brand.

'I get what I want,' he said with a calm decisiveness that made her toes curl up inside her white satin shoes.

'And that is?'

The smile that touched his beautiful mouth was slow and dangerous, making her shiver in the same moment that she felt a rush of heat through her veins, flooding her skin with colour.

'Oh, Amber, don't play the naïve innocent, it doesn't suit you—it never did. Isn't it obvious? I get you.'

'Me?' It was a sound of pure horror and revulsion, one that

should have provoked an equally passionate response from the man before her. But Guido just nodded, keeping that burning gaze targeted straight at her face.

'I get you. I've always wanted you and now I'll get you back in my life—and in my bed.'

Soft as they were, the words seemed to scrape away a much-needed protective layer from Amber's skin so that she felt weak and vulnerable, dangerously exposed.

'I only agreed to act as your wife—not really be that!' she protested vehemently, her voice echoing round the church. 'It won't be a real marriage!'

She might have felt that the fervour of her protest would reawaken the dark, flashing anger of moments before but instead it simply made that wicked, dangerous smile—that shockingly seductive smile—grow wider and more devastating.

'I'll settle for that—for now.'

'I won't sleep with you!'

The subtle emphasis on that 'for now' made her shift uneasily from one foot to another, facing the worrying thought that she had well and truly jumped out of the frying-pan and landed right in the heart of the blazing, red-hot fire.

'If that's a condition of your help—'

'It isn't,' Guido assured her, but then, just as she was allowing herself to relax just a little, he smiled again and went on, 'It doesn't need to be. I don't have to offer any ultimatums, or make conditions about this—I know you and I know how we are when we're together.'

The arrogant confidence of that assertion took Amber's breath away, leaving her gasping in disbelief.

'You'll stay with me for as long as is needed to let this whole *chiasso* over your attempt at a second marriage die down and while we're together you'll still be my wife. I'm sure you'll soon remember that the state of matrimony has its pleasures as well as its ties.'

'I won't—I'll never... '

The words shrivelled on her tongue as he took the couple of long strides that brought him to her, standing right in front of her and sliding one powerful hand under her chin, lifting it so that he was looking down into her face. The darkened eyes burned on her skin, the clean male scent of his body was all around her, and her mouth was so dry that she had to slick her tongue over her lips to moisten them.

'What is it they say about "never say never", hmm, *cara*? Because, believe me, in our case it will be true.'

'Nev...' Amber began but had to swallow down the word when he shook his dark head almost gently, that smile playing at the corners of his seductive mouth once again.

'Hush...' he murmured softly, laying one finger over her mouth to silence her. 'Don't say anything you might regret later. I'm happy to wait—for a while.'

His tone heavily underlined the ominous words.

'I know you will be worth waiting for. But I also know that you will find it harder than I ever will.'

With that restraining finger still on her lips, Amber didn't dare to speak, to protest, besides, she had no idea what she could say, what argument she might be able to drag up to refute his shocking assertion, his outrageous self-confidence. So she had to content herself with widening her eyes in a look of total disbelief, praying that her expression communicated the meaning she wanted.

But Guido simply ignored her silent refutation of his claim. Removing his finger and replacing it with his mouth, he pressed a slow, lingering kiss onto her partly open lips, taking her breath and all her composure with it as he did so.

Oh, how she wished she could control her reactions to his touch! She wanted to stay absolutely still, to show no response at all. To convince him by her behaviour that his kiss meant nothing to her. That she was immune to his touch...

But her treacherous body just wouldn't get the message that her terrified, rational brain was screaming at it. Instead of stiffening, her slender frame melted against his. Her mouth softened, letting his tongue slide tormentingly over her hungry lips, dip into the heat and moisture beyond them.

'You see, *bellissima*,' he murmured against her mouth, stealing another kiss as he drew breath to speak, 'I know you. And I know what you want.'

'I don't…' Amber tried but he shook his head and sealed off the words with another, deeper kiss, one that made her head swim, set her blood pounding.

'You don't want a cold-blooded English aristocrat like Rafe St Clair. You need a real man.'

'Like you, I suppose?' Amber wrenched her mouth away and tossed back her head to challenge him, green eyes blazing into bronze-rimmed black with what she hoped was daring defiance. She was struggling to deny her own senses, the yearning need that just his kiss, his touch had wakened in her all over again.

Guido smiled that tiger's smile again and ran his finger down the side of her face, along her neck and into the low V at the front of her dress, the curve of his lips growing as he watched the shuddering response she couldn't control.

'I can give you more than your water-in-his-veins Englishman can ever offer you. I can give you the passion you need, the sensuality you crave. I know what it was like between us; what it can be like again. I can—'

'No!' Amber actually stamped her foot hard on the flagstones, shaking her head so hard that her veil flew wildly around her head, yet more strands of chestnut hair escaping from the ornate style and dangling about her face. 'No, no, no! That isn't what I want and it isn't what's going to happen. What we had was a mistake—the worst mistake I've ever made in my life. It isn't going to happen again. I'd rather die than go back to that.'

'You, *carissima*, are a liar,' Guido told her softly. 'Your words are a lie—your protestation too. You lie even to yourself—and you don't do it terribly well. I shall enjoy proving your words to be untrue, even if it takes me some time. One day you will come to me, begging me to forget you ever said such things—and I…I will be waiting. The wait will be worth it—you will be worth it. Now…'

He held out his arm to her, obviously meaning her to take it.

'What?'

Still stunned by what he had said to her, the way he had dismissed her protest, Amber could only blink in stunned confusion.

'We are going to put the first part of our plan into action. We are going out there—as man and wife.'

'We—are?'

He still expected her to go with him, after what he'd just said? After the promise, the threat, he'd just made?

'Do you wish to back out of our agreement?'

Did she? And, more to the point, could she? Because if she didn't go with Guido, then that left her with—with nothing, she admitted to herself miserably. With nothing and no one. It was Guido or…

Silently she shook her head, flinching inwardly away from the grim satisfaction she saw in his face, the dark triumph that gleamed in his eyes.

'Then…'

Once more he held out his arm and this time she nerved herself to put her own arm in his, resting her hand on the hard strength of his forearm, feeling the tight power of muscle under her fingertips. The heat of his body seared her where her elbow was clamped against his side, pressed against the strong wall of his ribcage, sensing the heavy, regular beat of his heart so close by.

He had pushed his spare hand into his jacket pocket, pulling out a slim, silver-coloured mobile phone and flicking it open. With his thumb he pressed a single speed-dial button.

'What…?'

'I have a car waiting near by,' he told her before speaking into the phone, obviously issuing a string of instructions in fast, authoritative Italian. 'Franco will bring it to the gate—that way we will be able to get away as quickly as possible and so, hopefully, won't have to endure too much from the vultures outside.'

'But they're going to ask for a statement—something to explain all this... What are you going to say?'

'Leave that to me,' Guido told her, his tone deep and firm. 'Just follow my lead.'

And suddenly it was all that she wanted to do—to surrender herself to the strength of his body, the strength of his mind. To let him take control and handle everything as she knew he was more than capable of doing.

And if she had been able to think of anything for herself, or been able to act for herself, as soon as they started to move a sudden, flashing awareness slashed deep into her soul and took any last remaining ounce of strength from her, depriving her totally of the will to do anything.

As they walked down the aisle, arm in arm, towards the church door, she suddenly had a terrible, cruelly clear vision of just what they must look like to anyone seeing them there like that. She in her bridal finery, in the long white dress and the veil, the sweeping train that flowed from her waist at the back. And Guido in smartly tailored black, his head held high, his hand on her arm as he led her away from the altar and out towards the door at the end of the aisle.

Seen like this, anyone might take them for the bride and groom—the happy couple leaving the church after their wedding, starting out on a lifetime of happiness, a lifetime of love and sharing together as man and wife. And the image was so false, so deceptive, that it shrivelled her heart into ashes just to think of it.

And then, when she was least ready, least able to cope with it, her mind threw up another, even more painful memory. She saw herself as she had been a year before, on a late-winter day in Las Vegas. The whole wedding had been arranged in such haste, on such an impulse, that she had only a soft white cotton sundress to wear; no veil. Her only flower had been the single blood-red rose that Guido had given her as she got out of the taxi at the little wedding chapel he had booked for them to take their vows. She had had none of the silk and the lace that she wore now. No sweeping train, no fine tiara in her hair, but she had been so happy that day, so full of hope and joy for the future. Until the man she had married, the man who now walked beside her in a bitter parody of the walk of happiness of that day, had proved himself as false as she had come to believe that wedding to be.

Bitter, stinging tears burned in the back of her throat, pricked at her eyes, threatened to spill out wildly so that she had to keep blinking fiercely to hold them back. She couldn't see where she was going, had to rely on Guido to lead her, to get her to the door—to open it—and then she was outside, blinking in the blinding combination of sunlight and flashbulbs, hearing the click and whirr of cameras, the sudden shouts of interest, the litany of questions.

'Miss Wellesley—Amber...'

Tears blurred her eyes so that she couldn't see, she almost missed her footing and would have fallen down the stone steps if Guido hadn't reacted instantly, his strong arm coming round her, holding her tight at her waist, supporting her and half-carrying her along with him.

'A couple of questions...'

But this time there was a difference. This time she wasn't the only one who was in the firing line. It came as a shock to hear Guido's name, too, in the shouts and calls for attention.

'Just a word, Mr Corsentino...'

Halfway down the steps, Guido came to a halt, still holding her tightly. Automatically, she turned to him, confused by the sudden halt to their progress. But his eyes weren't on her; instead they were surveying the crowd around them, scanning the scene with cool control.

'I will issue a full statement later today that I hope will answer all your questions, but for now all you need to know is that my wife and I have reconciled. What happened here today shocked us into the realisation that we still care deeply for each other and we want to work towards a new future together. All we ask is that you give us a little peace and privacy to do so.'

To Amber's amazement the announcement seemed to work. Certainly, the buzz of questions seemed to lessen and, although the cameras still flashed, it was with less frenetic intensity.

She barely had a second to register it, for just at that moment a sleek and powerful car swept to a halt just outside the lych-gate.

That couldn't be...

But even as she formed the thought, Guido had tightened his grip on her waist and was striding through the group of newspaper men, taking her with him, whether she was ready or not.

She had a vague, blurry impression of a uniformed figure getting hastily out of the car and opening the door to the back seat for them, standing by while Guido helped her inside and then joined her on the soft leather seat. The door was slammed, the driver taking his own place and starting the engine before she had fully registered just what was happening.

A few seconds later they were on the road and speeding away from the church.

Guido sat back in his seat and raked both his hands through the black sleekness of his hair, before he turned those deep, burning eyes on her. There was no warmth in them, or showing on his face. Instead once again that cold, ruthless control that she had seen in the church was etched firmly onto his stunning features.

'Well, that is stage one,' he told her, his voice flat and emotionless. 'Now for stage two.'

CHAPTER FIVE

'WHERE are we going?'

It took Amber longer than he had anticipated to ask the question, Guido admitted. He had expected that the words would be the first thing out of her mouth as soon as they were away from the church. But instead she had surprised him by remaining silent for a good few minutes, seemingly turned in on herself, huddled in the corner, her eyes almost closed, her hands clasped together in her lap.

In fact, he had been so convinced that she had been shocked into speechlessness that he almost jumped when he heard her quiet voice and turned to see that she was sitting up more, her green eyes puzzled and a faint frown drawing her chestnut brows together as she considered the route they were taking, the countryside flashing past.

'I said, where are we going?' she repeated when he hesitated for a second. 'Where are you taking me?'

She wasn't going to like the answer, Guido reflected inwardly. In fact, he was pretty damn sure that their destination was going to be the very last place on earth that she wanted to be. But from the moment that she had agreed to come with him, he had decided that this was the way he wanted to play things and he had no intention of going back on that decision now.

'We're going to…' he began but then the way that the car

rounded a sudden bend in the road took away the need for any answer at all. Looking into Amber's face, he saw it change. Saw those big green eyes widen with shock, her soft pink mouth fall open in disbelief as she recognised the huge, elegant, white-painted building that lay ahead of them.

'No!'

For long, stunned seconds she simply stared, shaking her head in confusion and incredulity. Then:

'No!' She rounded on him in a fury. 'No way! This is the hotel where the wedding reception was supposed to be held!'

'I know—and it's where the—' he hunted for a suitable word '—the non-wedding reception is still being held. Franco told me that your would-be groom's parents have decided not to waste the cost of the banquet they had ordered for the wedding of their son and heir. They invited all their friends to come back here after the wedding was called off.'

'So why are we here?'

'I thought it would be a good idea to join them.'

'You thought!' Amber spluttered furiously. 'Well, you can just think again. There's no way on earth I'm going in there.'

'Oh, but you are.'

'I can't! They won't want to see me—in fact, I'm the last person on earth they would want to have appear at their—their wake for the wedding that never was. You saw what happened at the altar.'

'I saw.'

Guido's tone was dark as his thoughts as he remembered just how Rafe St Clair had reacted. The man was a hypocrite as well as a coward. Even if his own slate had been totally clean—which it wasn't—he still had no right to speak to any woman that way.

'Then you'll know that they're hardly going to welcome me with open arms—they're far more likely to slam the door shut in my face.'

'They won't do that because I am going in there with you.'

It was meant to reassure but it had the opposite effect. What little colour was left in her face fled from Amber's cheeks, making her eyes burn even more emerald-bright than ever.

'That will just make matters worse! Why are you doing this, Guido? What do you hope to gain from it?'

'Gain?' Guido queried sharply. 'I would have thought that was obvious. I want them to see that you are with me now.'

'Only until the furore dies down. And do you have to rub their noses in it?'

'Rub their…?'

Guido threw up his hands in exasperation at the impossibility of understanding some of the most peculiar of English phrases.

'If you mean that I want to make sure they realise the way things are now, then yes. Yes, I do. You are mine. The Press know that—the paparazzi know that—and now your high and mighty aristocratic friends will know it too.'

'Very few of them are my friends—even when I was going to marry Rafe, they weren't too keen on me. I was never into hunting, shooting and fishing—and they're definitely not going to be too friendly now. Guido, please…'

Impulsively she leaned forward, laying a hand on his arm.

'We don't have to do this. We can just go—get away quietly…'

Did she know what that did to him? Did she know how he felt as fierce need, burning hunger kicked in, hard and sharp, low down in his body, just at the touch of her hand? The warm, soft scent of her skin was a torment to his already heightened senses, and he felt as if he was drowning in the deep, deep pools of her eyes.

Only the thought that she knew only too well the effect she had on him—she had to know, damn it—stopped him from grabbing hold of her and pulling her onto his lap, crushing her mouth under his, kissing her stupid. She wasn't that naïve or that innocent. It was a deliberate ploy to distract him, to divert his attention from the plan he had in mind. And he wasn't going to let her get away with it.

'We aren't going anywhere quietly, *cara*,' he told her coldly. 'We are going to walk into that reception and let them see that you are my wife.'

'But I don't want to! I can't do it. We can just go…'

'Go where?' Guido snapped.

'Your house—wherever that is.'

'My home is in Sicily. And do you really think that you could travel all that way—take a flight in a plane—without your passport…and dressed like that?'

It took a moment for the impact of his words to hit home. Just for a second or two she stared at him blankly, obviously not knowing what he meant. But then she followed the direction of his gaze and a small, shocked sound escaped her throat.

Had she actually forgotten that she was still in full bridal finery? That she still wore the beautiful silk dress, the veil…?

Obviously she had because the eyes she now turned on his face again were shocked, clouded with consternation and uncertainty.

Did it ever cross her mind, as it had his so many times during the short journey, that to anyone on the outside, anyone who watched the car go past with the pair of them in it, must think that they were the bride and groom, leaving their wedding, heading for the reception?

Cold fury slashed at him at the contrast between the way it was now and the way it had been a year before, in Las Vegas. There, they had left the tacky little wedding chapel and driven back to her hotel with Amber giddy and giggling all the way. She had hung on to his arm as if she couldn't believe that he was real and for a while, he had let himself believe that was how she felt. He had tried to forget the moment in the ceremony when she had said, 'We've actually done it,' the change in her face as she'd said the words. He'd kissed her then; kissed away her doubts, he'd believed, and for a while they'd been happy. But then suddenly Amber had changed…

'You'll need to get out of those clothes, and your—what is

it you call it?—your going-away outfit is at the hotel, as are your passport, your cases.'

'How do you know that?'

Her uncertainty had left her in a rush and the green eyes were now noticeably sharper, definitely suspicious.

'How do you know where my things are?'

'Franco told me.'

A wave of his hand indicated the driver beyond the glass dividing panel. Franco was concentrating fiercely on the road, his attention tactfully anywhere but on his passengers.

'And how does Franco know?'

'I told him to make enquiries, as he has done since I first heard about this wedding. To find out what he could and report back to me.'

'To make enquiries!' Amber echoed indignantly, rejection sparking in her eyes. 'And report back! You've had me investigated?'

'*Naturalmente*. How do you think I knew details about your proposed wedding to St Clair? Do you think that I just happened to wander into the village on the right day, at the right time?'

If the truth was told, she hadn't thought about it at all, Amber admitted privately. She had been too shocked, too stunned by the explosive, blow to the head effect of his sudden appearance to even be able to consider what had led up to it and just why he was there. But now that she was forced to consider it, she didn't like what she was seeing at all.

'*Naturalmente!*' she echoed, putting all the horror she felt into the single word. '*Naturalmente!* I'll tell you something, Signor Corsentino. In Sicily it might be perfectly fine to spy on people and "make enquiries" about them—but to my mind it's not natural at all! In fact, I think it's hateful and offensive— an invasion of my privacy.'

'You'd prefer it if I'd stayed away and let you go ahead with your bigamous, illegal marriage?' Guido drawled, the gleaming mockery in his eyes only incensing her further.

'I would have preferred it if you'd stayed away, full stop!' she flung at him. 'Because of you, what was supposed to be the happiest day of my life has turned into the worst nightmare I've ever had.'

'And your first wedding day?' Guido slid the question in like a knife between her ribs. 'What was that, then? Surely that was supposed to have been the happiest day of your life?'

'The worst day of my life, more like!'

Amber was past caring what she said. She only knew she was desperate to score some much needed points on her side; to hit back for all the cruel punches he had already landed on her heart—her soul.

'The worst day—the biggest mistake—the stupidest thing I ever did in my life. If you must know, I hated every minute of it.'

'OK, I have the message,' Guido growled.

The car had swung into the long, curving drive up to the hotel door and as soon as it stopped he was out, pushing open the door without waiting for the uniformed commissionaire to step forward and do it. For a moment Amber thought that his black fury was going to drive him to stride straight into the building, not stopping to let her get out of the car to be with him.

But then he apparently rethought his actions, almost skidding to a halt on the gravel drive and turning to hold out a strong, tanned hand to her to help her out.

Amber's conscience stung her hard at the gesture. It was too late now to wish back the vicious words. She knew she'd lashed out in hurt, wanting to hurt, but that still didn't make them true. When she'd married him it had been the happiest day of her life. In fact, it hurt so much now to think of just how happy she had been then. It was only later that she had come to realise what a mistake she had made.

'Amber…'

Her hesitation was making him even more irritable. The hand that was held out to her moved in an imperious gesture, all but commanding her to stop messing about, take hold of it and get out of the car.

Knowing she had no choice but to co-operate—Guido was perfectly capable of reaching into the vehicle and hauling her out bodily if she tried his patience, which was obviously wearing very thin—Amber forced herself to take the help that was offered her, folding her fingers around his and letting him pull her towards the edge of the seat and then support her as she got to her feet.

And it was crazy, it was irrational, it was the most illogical thing in the world, but that simple touch suddenly changed everything. From shivering in the back of the luxurious vehicle, she suddenly felt flooded with courage, with new strength. The warm, hard power of Guido's touch, the ease with which he took her weight as she stood up, adjusted her balance, seemed to flow into her body too, straightening her spine and stilling the racing panic of her pulse.

And that feeling stabbed even harder at her already uncomfortable conscience.

'One thing,' Guido said curtly, his tone brutal, 'when we go in there, we go in as a team. We are together now and we act together, work on the story we agreed on. The story we have already told the Press. If by so much as a single glance, a single word, you do anything to turn that story into a lie then I will leave you there—alone with that pack of aristocratic vultures. Is that understood?'

'Perfectly.'

How could it be anything else? Without him she would have no protection, no help. She would be totally at the mercy of the people who had never thought her good enough to marry Rafe, and now would like her even less. Vultures, Guido had said, and 'vultures' described them perfectly. They would have no hesitation in attacking a wounded soul as soon as they saw her weakness.

'I understand.'

She was so close to Guido now that their bodies were almost touching. She could hear his breathing, breathe in the clean male scent of his body, look into the darkness of his eyes.

And when she did that the uneasy stinging of her conscience pushed her into hurried speech.

'And I'm sorry,' she said impulsively. 'Sorry for what I said.'

His carved, impassive expression didn't alter a bit. Not even a flicker of reaction showed in those deep-set eyes as he looked down into her anxious face.

'No matter,' he said dismissively. 'It is best to be honest. We are way past the time of pretending and saying only what we think the other wants to hear.'

And, turning, he caught her hand in his, holding it firmly so that she was forced to follow after him as he strode towards the huge double doors into the hotel. It was either that or be dragged along unceremoniously in his wake.

And so she followed.

She still didn't want to go into that hotel. She did not want to face Rafe and his family, possibly even her mother—least of all, her mother. She didn't see why they had to do it—other than for Guido's arrogant determination that the St Clairs should see that she was with him now, that she was his wife. That he, Guido Corsentino, had won the girl when their aristocratic candidate for her hand had well and truly lost out. If she could have done, she would have turned and run. Gone anywhere but here. But Guido was not going to let her do that, and right now he was the one in control. The one pulling the strings while she, as his puppet, danced to his demanding tune.

But at least with Guido beside her she was not facing this on her own.

From now on we're in this together, whether we like it or not, he had said and he was sticking firmly to his side of the bargain. *If she agreed to be his wife for as long as he demanded,* then he would be there, with her, supporting and protecting her as he had done when they had faced the band of reporters outside the church.

Besides, there were more practical reasons why she needed to go into the reception hotel, she remembered. Apart from the fact that she needed to change her clothes—to get out of this expensive and restricting bridal attire—there were also several things she needed if she was just to get on with her life. The passport Guido had mentioned—though the thought of travelling with him to that home in Sicily he had mentioned made her shiver inside—but also her bag with her purse, and all her money, her credit cards, her phone. That was still locked in the hotel room that had been assigned to her for the end of the reception, so that she could change and dress in her going-away outfit for the honeymoon she now was never going to enjoy.

So she took a deep, calming breath, brought her chin up and marched up the steps behind Guido, walked at his side through the imposing foyer, following the signs that read 'St Clair-Wellesley wedding reception.'

She only faltered when they reached the doors to the ballroom, where the buzz of conversation was so loud that it reached out into the corridor. Through the gold-decorated glass panels in the top halves of the doors, she could see the crowded room, filled with the people she and Rafe had invited to their wedding. The people who should now have been ready to enjoy the meal they had planned on, after she and her new husband had greeted them in a formal receiving line.

Instead of which she was now standing outside, looking in, an intruder at her own wedding celebration, still in her wedding dress, but with her hand in that of a totally different man—the man who, in the eyes of the law, if not in her heart, was actually her true husband.

'Don't tell me you've changed your mind! It's too late for that.'

For a moment, Amber didn't realise where the words had

come from. She only registered the cold fury in them, the way they were hissed at her in a dark undertone from behind, making her jump like a nervous cat. But even as she spun round she recognised the voice with a sinking heart.

'Mother…'

But Pamela Wellesley wasn't listening. Instead, her face drawn into a pale, tight mask of cold fury, she waved an elegantly manicured hand in the direction of the scene beyond the glass door.

'Have you seen them all in there? Well, have you? That's where we could be—where we *should* be, if you hadn't lost the little sense you had inside your stupid head! They wouldn't let me in and it's all your fault.'

'But I…' Amber began but before she could get the words out Guido had taken a step forward. Just a single step but it brought Pamela's gaze to him, her eyes widening as she looked up into his stern, unyielding face. Amber could have sworn that her mother had actually been unaware of his presence just for a moment because she had been so intent on spilling out her fury at the way she believed her daughter had ruined all her plans.

'If you want to blame anyone, then I suggest you blame me.'

'You!' Pamela choked now.

'Me,' Guido confirmed with an easy calm, one that was belied by the tightness Amber could see in his strong jaw, the way his eyes were narrowed as they focused on the older woman's face.

'You're here!'

'Of course.'

He kept his tone soft and almost pleasant. But it only needed that to give the game away. Hearing it made Amber shiver faintly in recognition of just what he was holding back and what, she recognised with slightly stunned disbelief, kept even her mother quiet as their eyes clashed in silent confrontation.

'Where else would I be but at my wife's side?'

'Your…' Pamela began then spluttered to a halt. 'It's true then. You're married…'

'We're married. And you might as well know—because you'll read it in the papers tonight—that we've decided to try again. Have another go at making our marriage work. That means we're a couple—and so anything you have to say to Amber, you say to me as well.'

There was no threat in the words, no aggression. There was only a cold, hard certainty that sliced through her mother's assurance, making her gaze falter, her eyes flicker in uncertainty as they went to her daughter's face.

'Is this true?'

Amber didn't need the small warning squeeze of her hand to remind her of the bargain they had made; the way that she had agreed to let the world think that they were back together.

'Perfectly true.' She was surprised at the depth of confidence she managed to inject into her voice. 'Guido and I are together. My future is with him.'

It sounded so good. It sounded so real—when all the time it was nothing but a lie. It sounded so much like her dream of a year before that it tore at her heart, making her eyes burn, her throat close so that she couldn't have said another word.

She didn't have to. Already her mother was backing down, backing away. Her angry gaze took in the two of them then obviously decided against taking any risks.

'I wish you joy of each other,' she snapped, turning on her heel. 'But don't come running to me when it all goes wrong.'

'Oh, I won't.' Amber didn't care if she was heard or not. She needed to say it for herself. 'I won't…' she repeated as she watched her mother disappear down the corridor.

It was only when Pamela turned a corner out of sight that she drew in a long, uneven breath and squared her shoulders.

'So now what?'

'One down, one to go.' He indicated the door and the party beyond. 'Ready?'

Guido could feel the tension in Amber's body just through the link of their joined hands. He'd have to be totally insensitive not to be aware of the way that it had been growing stronger with each step they took towards the ballroom reception. And the confrontation with her witch of a mother had been the last straw. So now a swift glance down at her face showed the way that she had lost every last trace of colour, her skin so pale it was almost translucent. Her sharp white teeth were worrying at the softness of her bottom lip, digging in so hard that he almost expected to see bright pearls of blood spring to the surface at any moment.

'Don't!'

Concern made the word sharper than he'd intended, bring her brilliant emerald gaze up in a rush.

'Amber—no...'

His tone was one of reproach but his touch was gentle as he reached out to place his fingers over her mouth to stop her from inflicting the small, unthinking damage on herself.

'No, *cara*,' he said again, more softly this time, and saw her eyes widen even more in disbelief and shock.

He didn't blame her. She must be wondering what had happened to the coldly blazing fury of just minutes before. The rage that had erupted when he had been forced to face just how little her wedding to him had meant; how much she regretted ever having married him. She had flung those facts in his face with the deliberate intention of provoking him, and, like a fool, he'd let his reaction show.

But now, suddenly, all that heat, all that anger had gone. And the truth was that he didn't know where or how it had seeped away. But he sure as hell knew why.

It had started in the moment that she had stood up to her mother by declaring them a couple, but more than that, it was touching her that had been his downfall.

At the moment that his fingers had touched the lush, yielding softness of her mouth, it had been as if someone had yanked out a plug somewhere so that all the stored-up anger and bitterness inside him had drained away, leaving only room for the intense jag of sensuality that arced through his body, pooling low down in his groin.

Having touched her, so very softly, he now found that he just couldn't pull away again. His fingers stayed on her mouth, his thumb tracing the sweet shape of it, stroking over the fresh rose swell of her slightly parted lips, sliding between them.

On his hand he felt the cooler air of her snatched-in breath, the warm moistness of her inner mouth. And he could have sworn that, just for a split second, her tongue slipped up and out, to taste his skin as it rested against hers.

He had vowed to himself that he would drag her, kicking and screaming, into that room if he had to. That he would make her face Rafe St Clair with him, as his wife, even if he had to force her every step of the way. But suddenly that resolution escaped from him in a rush, like air from a pricked balloon.

'Are you OK?'

Her expression showed that it had shocked her almost as much—no, more—to hear the question as he had shocked himself by asking. Clearly she had read his intent in his face and now she couldn't believe that he was actually concerned about the way she felt.

'I…' she began but then the words failed her and he couldn't tell if it was because she wasn't OK, or if the movement of her mouth on the words had brought her lips and tongue into contact with the skin of his thumb again, and the sensation was what had driven the words from her mind, made the words die in her throat.

Her pupils had widened, seeming to fill the whole of her irises so that there was only the smallest rim of green around the edges, and under his restraining fingers the pulse at her wrist kicked up suddenly, fast and erratic, making her breath catch unevenly.

'Guido...' she tried again, her tone pleading, her voice low. But he shook his head to silence her

'You can do this,' he told her. 'Don't forget, I'll be with you. At your side. You're not alone.'

And to reinforce his words, to drive that point home, he bent his head and took her lips, replacing the soft pressure of his fingers with the firm demand of his mouth. He meant only to deliver a brief caress then move away but, as before, as soon as his mouth touched hers he knew such a twist of hunger, hard and hot and savage, that he had to fight against the need to grab at her there and then, pull her close, crush her against him.

He couldn't even blame the fury in his blood on the way that she responded to him. Because she didn't respond but simply took his kiss with calm compliance, her mouth lying passive under his, her lips warm and soft but unresponsive, not opening under his, giving nothing, just accepting.

And it was because she didn't respond that he had the devil's own trouble controlling himself.

He wanted her to respond—needed to make her respond. He wanted to take her mouth so hard, so strong—so softly, so enticingly—each and every possible way he could so that she was forced to respond to him—to open to him. It outraged him that she could stand there, so calm and submissive, giving nothing, when inside the claws of lust were threatening to rip him in two.

But now was not the time. Already the uniformed major domo provided by the hotel had spotted them and, opening the door, was looking at them enquiringly. He even gave a discreet little cough to get their attention.

With a savage effort, Guido wrenched himself away from the kiss and turned just in time to see the man's obvious astonishment and confusion.

'I'm sorry...' he began stumblingly. 'I thought...'

His bewildered eyes went to Amber, taking in the long white dress and the veil.

'Mr St Clair is already here,' he said, frowning in puzzlement. 'I understood…'

'It's all right,' Guido reassured him. 'There's been a change of plan.'

Stepping forward, he murmured swift instructions in the man's ear. A generous tip slipped into his hand eased some of the remaining discomfort in his face.

'You understand?'

'Yes, sir.'

With a curt nod of satisfaction, Guido turned back to Amber.

This was it, he told himself. This was when he put into place the last part of his plan to make sure that Amber and the St Clair family parted for ever and went their separate ways. After this, there would be no chance at all that they would want her to marry any one of them. And that was exactly how he'd planned it.

After tonight, Amber Wellesley would be all his.

'Come…'

Once more her hand was enclosed in his. Once more she was obliged to move forward with him or risk embarrassment.

The double doors to the ballroom were flung open and, with Amber stumbling apprehensively at his side, Guido strode forward to stand firmly in the middle of the carpeted landing at the top of the short flight of stairs that curved its way down into the huge blue and gold ballroom.

And there he stopped. Stood still and silent, his spine straight, his shoulders back, dark head held arrogantly high.

Stood and watched and waited as first one person and then another noticed their arrival. Conversations died. Women elbowed each other in the ribs to draw their attention to what was happening. Men stared then nodded furiously in the direction of the sight.

And like the sea rushing away on an ebbing tide, the buzz

of chatter stilled, a deathly silence fell, and eventually every eye in the room was turned on them.

Only when the silence was complete did Guido move. Turning slightly towards the man who was hovering at his back, he gave another small, commanding nod.

Immediately the *maître d'* moved forward, cleared his throat.

'Ladies and gentlemen!' he announced into the frozen silence, his words seeming to make the air shatter as he spoke. 'I give you—the—the bride and groom. Mr and Mrs Guido Corsentino.'

CHAPTER SIX

'THIS is your room, madam.'

'Thank you.'

Amber waited until the maid who had shown her to the room on the second floor of the hotel had retreated before she slid the key card into the lock and waited for the light to turn green.

She had just endured the worst few minutes of her life. She had been peered at, examined, looked up and down.

She had had to watch in disbelief as, on Guido's orders, bottles of vintage champagne appeared from the hotel's cellars and were opened. Glasses were filled with a lavish hand, and to her horrified amazement Guido announced that he hoped that everyone there would drink a toast, 'To my reunion with my beautiful bride.'

They were frightened of him, she realised on a sense of mind-blowing shock. Terrified of what he might do and—yes—there was a little touch of admiration there, a grudging respect that kept their tongues on the right side of civil, no matter what their minds might have been thinking.

In his all-black outfit, Guido prowled amongst them like a sleek black panther wandering lazily through a huge flock of birds of paradise. A sleek black smiling panther who was obviously enjoying himself while they all waited and watched, frozen in apprehension, not daring to make a move in case it was the wrong one and drove the jungle cat to pounce with deadly intent.

But Amber couldn't find any cause for enjoyment of anything in the whole ordeal. To her, every second was an endurance test, her worst nightmare ever come true and actually existing in the real world. She didn't even have the hope that she might wake and find it all behind her. To make matters worse, the elegant white satin shoes were beginning to pinch unmercifully, a brutal, pounding ache had set up in her head, and she felt as if someone had put a hard steel band around her temples and was slowly twisting it tighter and tighter.

So it was with a rush of intense release that she saw Guido beckon one of the staff to him and obviously make some sort of request. A moment later he had come close to her, touched her lightly on the arm.

'It's time you left now,' he said in a tone that made it clear it was not a suggestion but a command. 'This young lady will take you to your room—where your clothes and your cases are. Get changed and wait for me there.'

She had been so relieved at being released, at escaping from the torment of the reception that should have been hers and Rafe's but that had, like her wedding, been hijacked and completely overturned by Guido's intervention, that she fled from the room, like a bird freed from its cage, seeking the sanctuary of the haven provided for her.

'Well, you have done well for yourself, haven't you?' a drawling voice said close by, jolting her out of her thoughts and making her look up into a familiar pair of cold blue eyes.

Of course. Rafe must have left his going-away clothes in the room next door and by some appalling stroke of fortune he had been coming out of his room just as she had reached hers. He had already changed out of his formal morning coat and was now dressed in the elegantly cut suit and silk shirt he had planned to travel in.

'I don't know what you mean.'

Amber tried twisting the door handle, but the light on the lock had already gone out. She would have to take out the key card and insert it once again.

'She doesn't know what I mean,' Rafe echoed cynically, coming close and lounging back against the wall. 'Why, setting yourself up with a handsome Italian billionaire who could buy us all in the blink of an eye, of course. If that's not doing well for yourself, I don't know what is. So tell me,' he went on, not giving her a chance to speak, or even to think. 'Was that what our marriage was all about, hmm? A way of bringing him to heel after you'd split up?'

'Of course not,' Amber insisted.

She'd no way of knowing where he'd got the idea that Guido was a billionaire, but she had to put him right on that. But Rafe wasn't interested in listening to her. All he cared about was the sound of his own voice.

'Well, you may have just done me a favour too, in the end, so I reckon we'll just call it quits.'

And then, to her total shock and consternation, he did the last thing she had expected. Looking straight into her face, he actually smiled, though it was the most peculiar, most alien smile that Amber had ever seen. It hadn't touched his eyes, which had remained as cold and ice-blue as a frozen floe in the Arctic.

'At least with my heart having been broken so publicly this way,' he went on, resting one long-fingered hand on the breast pocket of his elegant jacket just above where the heart in question lay, 'no one will expect me to even think about marrying another woman for some time. And that suits me perfectly. So enjoy your Italian, darling—and I'll enjoy my freedom.'

And with an airy wave he was gone, stepping swiftly into the lift and shutting the door right in her face.

Amber was still standing staring at the polished lift doors in shock, when the second lift just near by arrived at the second floor, opened, and Guido stepped out onto the green-carpeted corridor. A dark frown creased the space between his brows when he saw her.

'You're not ready. You've not even started to get changed.'

Guido's tone was sharp and, coming on top of her private thoughts, it caught right on a raw edge of an exposed nerve.

'Just because I'm your wife, it doesn't mean I have to jump when you click your fingers.'

And then, because it was the question that was uppermost in her mind, the one that just wouldn't stop fretting at her thoughts—

'Why, Guido? Tell me why.'

At least he had the grace not to pretend he didn't know what she meant. But he moved to unlock the door to her room, taking her by the arm and hurrying her into it before he stopped to answer her.

'I told you—I wanted them to see you were with me. That you're my wife.'

Amber crossed to the big, high, king-sized bed and sank down on it with a long, low sigh that was a blend of exhaustion and total despair

'Wouldn't the pictures in the paper tomorrow—and your "statement" tonight—have done the job as well?'

'I don't think so. I wanted them to see it with their own eyes. And I wanted to see their faces when I did so.'

'You mean that you wanted to parade me in front of them like some sort of trophy!'

'If you choose to see it that way,' Guido dismissed her anger carelessly.

'And what possible other way is there to see it?'

'That I wanted to make sure they never got their hands on you again.'

'Did you really think that after what happened, Rafe would even consider asking me to marry him again?' Amber couldn't hide her incredulity and it rang sharply in her voice.

'He'll have to come through me first.'

'Well, from the way that Rafe just behaved I have very little doubt that isn't going to happen.'

'The way that…'

Guido's head went back, his eyes narrowing sharply.

'Has he said something?' he demanded harshly. 'Hurt you?'

'Hurt me? No, he didn't hurt me but…I think I need to talk to him.'

'No!'

Moving further into the room, Guido kicked the door behind him, heard it slam and the lock click into place.

'You will not speak to St Clair!'

But his tone had been too hard, his attitude too forceful. He could see it in the way that her chin came up, defiance flashing in her eyes, her jaw firming stubbornly.

'And why not?'

'Because I asked you to come up here to change your clothes so that we could leave as soon as possible.'

'You didn't ask—you ordered.'

'And you really want to spend the rest of the day dressed up like a pantomime princess.'

'You don't like this dress?'

He'd intrigued her now and he welcomed the way it distracted her thoughts from wandering down paths he didn't want her to follow. She smoothed a hand over the silken skirts of her wedding gown, frowning thoughtfully.

'It's very beautiful,' Amber said.

'I preferred the dress you wore for our wedding.'

'That simple thing? It was just something I'd picked up from a chain store.'

But she'd looked amazing in it. She had looked so sweet and innocent, excited and yet nervous, anticipating her wedding day with such joy that it was just bubbling out of her. At least, that was what he had thought at first.

It was only later that he had realised how much she regretted what she had done, when a better opportunity—a more aristocratic suitor—a wealthier suitor, she believed—had come along.

'This is a designer original—it cost a small fortune. I would never have been able to afford it by myself, of course. But Rafe offered to pay for it…'

'He did what?'

It was the last thing Guido wanted to hear. He detested the idea of anything that man had provided touching her. The thought of Rafe St Clair sent his blood pressure spiking, made him feel nauseous with fury. Though that was nothing to the way he had felt when he had first learned just whom St Clair planned to marry.

But then, why was he surprised? Hadn't she left him for just that sort of reason? Because she wanted the sort of man who could provide her with designer originals? He had never been more thankful that he hadn't told her the full truth about himself. If he had, then she might have stayed with him for all the wrong reasons.

'Take it off!'

'What?' Her eyes widened in shock.

'Take that dress off.'

'With you standing there?' Amber shook her head sharply. 'No way! At least have the decency to leave the room.'

If he went out that door, he wouldn't stop until he found St Clair and ripped his head from his shoulders, the way he was feeling right now. Fighting the urge to do just that, Guido flung himself down in the chair that stood in the wide bay window.

'I'm your husband and there's nothing I haven't seen. Take it off, Amber, or I'll tear it off you myself.'

The look she flung him was one of total loathing but he let it bounce off the shield of restraint he had put up around himself. Whether Amber liked it or not, staying was definitely the safer option.

Or was it?

With another blazing, fulminating glare in his direction, Amber got to her feet and deliberately turned her back on him. Once again he was presented with the view of her he had seen as he entered the church. And once again he knew the twisting, primitive hunger low down in his gut.

It was worse this time. Worse in so many ways.

Then he had only seen her back view, in the white silk dress, with the long lace veil falling down from the crown of her head. He hadn't seen her, hadn't spoken to her, hadn't touched her for months. But the long-ago memories had been bad enough.

Now he had newer memories to add to those long-ago ones. Now he was tormented by the recollection of how it had felt to hold her in his arms, to know the soft, warm pressure of her slender frame up against his; how it had felt to kiss her. If he slicked his tongue over his lips he could still taste the sweetness of her there. The scent of her perfume was still in his nostrils.

And the claw of lust was harder than ever before.

'Want any help?' Guido offered.

'No!'

Did she know what she was doing to him with those small, sensual, wriggling movements? Rationally, he knew they were designed to enable her to reach the handle of the long zip at the back of the dress, ease it down. But the effect they were having on him was very, very far from rational.

She'd got the damned zip down partway now. Far enough down to reveal the bones and lace of some corset type of underwear. Underwear that exposed the delicate pink of her skin above and that skimmed downwards towards the narrow line of her waist, the sensual swell of her hips. And still she kept up those little movements, twisting, arching her back as she struggled to reach the bit right in the middle of her back.

'Are you sure?'

'Positive. You come near me and I'll— Ouch!'

It was a sharp, instinctive cry of pain and it had him out of his chair in a second, taking a step forward hastily and then freezing sharply, trying to assess the situation; see what had happened.

Amber too had stilled, one hand halfway up her back from below, the other reaching from her shoulder, both of them straining for and not quite reaching the small white handle of the fine zip fastener. Her head was also pulled slightly back, held at an unnatural angle.

'The veil has caught in the zip. That's why it won't move down.'

'I know!' It was a sound of frustrated exasperation, hissed out from between gritted teeth. 'But I can manage.'

'Of course you can.' He deliberately laced the words with sarcasm.

'I can—I just need to… Ouch!'

And then it came, muffled, uneven, and very low.

'Guido…please…'

He was at her side in a moment, bending to the spot where the delicate lace of her veil had snagged in the runners of the zip fastening. He could see now why she had been exclaiming in pain. Not only had the veil caught, but it was pulled tight, dragging her head back, tugging against the ornate hairstyle, the fine tiara too, in a way that must have been desperately uncomfortable. And each time she moved she only entangled herself further, adding to her discomfort.

'Hold still.'

The best thing to do was to remove the tiara and the veil. With them loose…

His fingers were busy as his thoughts, reaching for and pulling out the hundreds of pins, or so it seemed, that held the headdress in place. Soft tendrils of hair fell about his hands as he worked. They stroked his face in silken caresses, soft as the touch of her hands. The heated scent of her body rose up to surround him, tugging on his senses, making him even harder than before so that he swore softly and savagely in his own language.

'What?'

Amber heard him mutter but the sound was muffled by the way he had his head bent, his attention apparently focused on disentangling her from the veil and the headdress.

'What did you say?'

No answer. He really was concentrating on what he was doing. And for that she should be grateful.

If he was absorbed in extricating her from the tangled veil and headdress, then he wouldn't notice the way her colour came and went as heat suffused her body and then fled from it, leaving her cold and shivery as if she was in the grip of a fever. Her heart was pounding so hard that she was sure he must hear it, even through the boned and stiffened basque she wore underneath the silk dress. Her breath was ragged and uneven, and her head swam so that she swayed uncertainly on her feet, her eyes staring, unfocused, at the opposite wall.

His touch on her hair was soft but sure; it felt like a caress even though she knew that was not what he meant it to be.

Admit it! she reproached herself. Admit that you want it to be a caress. That you have wanted him to touch you—to caress you—ever since that kiss in the church.

That kiss.

Her skin flamed, her senses yearning, just to remember it. It was as if that kiss had swept away all the intervening days and months since she had walked out on Guido and their marriage. She had spent a long year trying to get over him and it had taken just one touch, one kiss and she was right back where she had started. Back in the yearning hunger, the demanding passion that his touch sparked in every nerve in her body. Back in the throes of the powerful sexual need that this man—and only this man—could awaken in her.

She'd grabbed back the vulnerable heart she'd given him,

and guarded it from him ever since she had discovered his duplicity and his callousness, but the truth was that she was only safe from her sexual enslavement to Guido Corsentino while he was thousands of miles away, safely out of her life.

He had merely to walk back into her world and she was lost again. Adrift on a heated sea of longing and need without a compass or any sort of guiding star. The only recognisable landmark on her horizon was Guido himself. And, like the compass needle that was always pulled to the north, she was drawn to him whether she wanted to be or not.

CHAPTER SEVEN

'STAY still, *cara*,' Guido advised as the shocking realisation made her jump nervously, wanting to jerk away from his touch and yet longing to stay right where she was. 'Almost done… There.'

The release of the pull on her scalp told Amber that the veil was free, the headdress off and she sighed in relief as she felt it fall to the floor. But the next moment the sense of tension was back again, but in a very different way. This time it was screaming through every nerve of her body as Guido straightened up and, instead of moving away, took a step closer.

He was still behind her and she could feel the heat from his body reaching out to her, surrounding her. Where the back of her dress hung open, revealing her shoulders, her spine, she could feel tiny prickles of awareness start to shiver over her skin in anticipation of a touch she yearned for so much that she could almost will herself to feel it.

'Thank you,' she managed, her voice croaking.

'*È niente…*'

It was so soft it was just a breath, a warm breath that feathered along every nerve, whispered over the exposed flesh of her back. She felt her throat close, her mouth dry. She couldn't have moved if she tried. But she didn't want to try.

Touch me! her mind screamed silently. Please, please, touch me!

self-preservation. She didn't know what drove her, didn't understand what pushed her forward, only knew that it was an impulse, a need she couldn't resist.

She was hungry, yearning and empty inside, aching with a need that his touch had awoken, his kisses had brought spiralling to the surface. She had felt his mouth on her skin, his touch on her body. Now she needed, so desperately, to kiss and touch and taste and feel for herself.

Needed to kiss and touch and taste and feel the essence that was purely Guido.

Before her brain had even registered the thought, she had taken the couple of steps forward that brought her up close to him. Her breathing fast and shallow, her mind spinning, she lifted her head, pressed her mouth to the hard plane of his cheek, feeling the raw scrape of stubble against the sensitive flesh of her lips.

He smelled wonderful; he tasted even better. She let her tongue slip out; let it touch against his skin. Tasted the slightly salt flavour of him.

And saw his eyes fly open, look down into hers.

If she had thought that they seemed to have been turned black by desire before, now they were even deeper and darker than ever. But they gleamed like burnished metal, burning into hers with hungry fire.

Just for a moment that hunger startled her, made a quiver of something that was close to fear run through her. Never before, even when they were married, had he shown so openly, so shockingly, the searing passion he felt for her. It terrified her in the same moment that it excited her, so that she made to take a step back…

And stopped dead as his arm came out, fastening around her neck, pulling her closer. His mouth came down on hers, crushing it, taking it, making her his again.

That was the only thought that went through her head before

her mind stopped functioning and sensation took over. *I'm his and only his. I don't want anyone else. Don't want to be with anyone else. This is what I want—this is what I need.*

This is what I am.

But the next kiss drove any rational thought from her head. The fierce, sizzling strength of it took her mind and shattered it, left her only able to function on the most basic, most primitive level. The level of pure physical need and nothing more.

Her mouth opened under his, allowing the silken heat of his tongue to invade and plunder, taking, tasting, teasing, tantalising. And she went right with it. Giving back everything she could in return, matching need for need, hunger for hunger.

She barely noticed when Guido snatched her up. Wasn't aware of the way that he shrugged off his jacket as he carried her towards the bed. Her arms were clasped tight around his neck, her mouth locked with his as they fell together onto the gold-coloured covers, her shoes tumbling to the floor as they did so.

'It's been too long...too long...way too long...' Guido muttered as he kissed his way along her jawline, over her cheek, back to her mouth.

He didn't stop to ask if it was what she wanted too. Didn't need to. They both knew the question had been asked, the answer given in that first moment when she'd turned to him. And again when she had let the dress drop. And when she had stepped into his space, kissed him on the cheek. From that point on there had been no going back and both of them knew it.

'I have waited too long...'

'Mmm...'

It was all that Amber could manage, the unformed sound catching in her throat as he came down on top of her, his mouth taking hers again, hands roaming over her body, seeking, stroking, finding pleasure spots she had forgotten existed, ones she could have sworn that even she hadn't known about before. Excitement rushed through her, fizzing, burning, stinging like an electric current, making her tug hard at his shirt, wrench the buttons from their fastenings.

'I'm wearing too many clothes…' It was a moan of complaint, of protest, and she felt rather than heard the dark laughter that shook his long body.

'Too many clothes, perhaps,' he told her huskily, 'but then again, I think I like it. I like this amazing contraption you're wearing—love the way it pushes your breasts out—everything on display for my eyes…'

They burned into her skin, his gaze almost a physical touch in itself.

'My hands…'

Hot fingers stroked the exposed pale flesh of her breasts, curving over them, cupping them above and then below, lifting them even higher.

'And my mouth…'

Suiting action to the words, he bent to the soft skin, letting first his lips, then his tongue slide over her quivering breasts, finally letting his teeth graze the delicate curves, making her moan aloud in excitement.

His hands were at her sides, moving over the boned bodice, shaping the narrow curve of her waist. Then up again, his touch growing heavier, more urgent, hard fingers slipping into the lacy cups, finding her swollen nipples, rolling them between a forefinger and thumb.

'Guido…!'

His name was a gasp of shock, a sound of delight, a moan of encouragement all in one.

'You like that, *mia bellezza*?'

Guido punctuated the words with hot kisses over the curve of one breast and then the other, then back again.

'You want more?'

'Oh, yes…yes…I want…I want you.'

'Soon, *carissima*, soon.'

Another kiss took her yearning mouth, giving her something of what she needed and yet promising so much more that it fed her hunger even as it appeased it.

'First…'

Hooking his thumbs over the lacy edge of the white silk basque, he pulled it down, exposing her breasts to his arousing touch and his even more exciting mouth. Moaning aloud again, Amber moved her head restlessly on the fine cotton of the pillows, arching her back, pressing herself against his mouth so that the sensations were increased, making her head spin with pleasure.

But she didn't just want to feel. She wanted to touch, to match him caress for caress. She wanted to know the heat and softness of his skin, to have the power of his muscles, the hardness of bone under her fingertips.

'Too many clothes…' she muttered again complainingly, her hand clutching at his shirt, tugging, twisting, trying to wrench it from him.

'*Impaziente…*' Guido muttered, laughter once again threading through his voice.

But he helped her out, shrugging off the loosened shirt, and somehow still managing to concentrate his attention on the tightened, aching breasts he had exposed. The feel of his hot skin, the bunched muscles, made Amber sigh with delight and she let her hands roam where they could. Under her caresses, Guido's spine arched, burning eyes closed.

'Talking of too many clothes…these have to go.'

Through the heated delirium that filled her head, Amber barely noticed the feel of his strong fingers closing over the fine lace that was her only covering at the most intimate spot between her thighs. There was a swift, hard tug, the sound of material ripping and her eyes opened wide in shock at the realisation of what had happened.

'Guido…'

But Guido showed no sign of any sense of guilt, or even

concern as he smiled down into her stunned face and kissed the stunned protest from her lips as he tossed the tattered remnants of her knickers carelessly to one side.

'I'll buy you a dozen more—a hundred…' he promised against her mouth. 'Besides, they were in my way.'

To prove his point, he trailed his knowing hand down her body, following the lines of one of the boned strips that stiffened the corset to the point where it ended just on her waist. From there he let it wander even lower, tracing a path of fire through the curls that hid her femininity, slipping between her thighs, easing them apart. With practised ease he found the tiny, swollen spot that was burning with a hungry need for just this moment and stroked a soft caress over its throbbing tip.

With her body already ablaze with longing as a result of his enticing attentions elsewhere, that single touch was enough to have Amber convulsing underneath him, crying out his name in the heat of her need.

'Guido—Guido—please…'

Her vision was hazed with passion but she caught the quick flashing smile that showed his delight at her response, the triumph he didn't try to hide.

'I knew it would be this way… Knew how it would be between us…'

Knew…

Just for a second, his muttered satisfaction stilled Amber, as a cold shaft of something uncomfortable and disturbing almost but not quite reached through to Amber's rational mind. But just as a flicker of awareness of something she wanted to resist, to armour herself against, threatened to pierce the heated haze of delight, Guido stroked her again, his touch knowing, tormenting, even more arousing than before. Instantly, the flames of passion swept over her, taking with her that momentary doubt as she clung to him, melting into him, not knowing where she ended and he began.

Long, powerful legs edged between her own, easing them apart. She felt the strength of muscle even through the delicate covering of the stockings she still wore, the fine material of his trousers. She heard her blood thunder in her veins as the heated hardness of him nudged against the sensitised core of her body.

'You're mine,' he whispered in her ear, rough and thick and disturbingly raw. 'Mine. You always have been and you always will. This is how it was in the past, how it is and how it will be in the future. *Si? Si?*'

'Yes…'

It was all that Amber could manage. All she could force from her, dry mouth, her parched throat. The heat of her need seemed to be burning her up, shrivelling her brain in its fire.

'Oh, yes …'

She didn't want to think—didn't want him to wait. Even the seconds of hesitation that he kept her waiting ticked in an agony of frustration. Impatiently she moved, shifting underneath him, bringing her hips up slightly, opening herself to him even more.

'Ah, yes, *belleza*…'

Firm hands clamped on her hips, hard fingers digging into the swell of her buttocks. In one smooth, powerful movement, he raised her slightly, positioned himself in just the right spot and thrust, hard and long, deep, deep inside her.

'Gui—' Amber began but he caught her cry in his own mouth as he sealed her lips with his. And kept them closed while his powerful body worked its primitive magic on hers.

At first his movements were in total control, each hard, fierce movement, each thrust inwards taking her close—so close—to the wild peak of fulfilment but then slowly, agonisingly, letting her down again, holding her, tantalising her…before he moved again. And each time Amber had to bite down hard on her lower lip as frustration stung at her, the sensation of being so near and yet so far an agony of disappointment at the same time as it seared a further brand of delight on her already shuddering body.

But then, in the space of a heartbeat, it seemed, even his iron control snapped. The slow, deliberate rhythm fractured, became harder, faster, fiercer. The primitive power of passion overtook him, shattering his command of his senses, of his body, and with a harsh, wild cry of abandonment he gave in to the force of need that took them both out of the world they knew and into a space of light and heat and pure, uncontrollable sensation.

Her name was a harsh shout, mingling with her own cry of ecstasy as they reached the peak and fell from it, tumbling into the darkness of oblivion in perfect unison.

Amber had no idea how long it was before the total devastation of her senses started to ease, to ebb away so that she could hear and feel again. She still felt blinded, too numbed to find the energy to open her eyes, to even try to see, and so it was as she lay in total darkness, exhausted, satiated, unable to move, that she felt Guido stir, rolling his heavy body from hers and coming to lie beside her on the bed.

She heard his sigh, deep and satisfied, but blended with a dark thread of rough laughter that pricked at her uncomfortably, sending a quiver of unease right through her body.

'Never say never,' Guido muttered softly, his voice still thick with the aftermath of the passion that had shaken him to his core. 'Oh, *cara, cara*—never, ever say never.'

CHAPTER EIGHT

THIS was not supposed to have happened.

Guido sighed, low and deep, as he flung his head back against the pillow and closed his eyes again. Raking both hands through his hair, he faced the fact that he had probably just made one of the biggest, most stupid mistakes of his life.

This was damn well not supposed to have happened.

Not here, not now. Not like this. Not yet…

And not, most definitely not, when he was not prepared. When he had no protection with him, and even if he had, would not have had the presence of mind, the control, to even think of using it.

And not just physical protection either.

'Dannazione…' The curse and others more violent, much more basic in his own language slipped from him as he looked the facts squarely in the face and acknowledged what a stupid bloody mess he had made of things.

So much for taking things slowly.

So much for waiting and seeing, watching, learning. So much for acting on his thoughts, his intelligence rather than his libido.

So much for thinking at all.

At his side, Amber lay, limp with exhaustion, her eyes closed, her limbs splayed over the bed.

Asleep? Dear God, he hoped so. He prayed so.

He needed time to recover; time to get his body and his mind back under control. He needed time to work out just what he'd done by acting without thought, without any consideration of the consequences. Without looking ahead into the future at all.

He needed time to decide just where the hell they went from here.

Forcing his eyes open, he turned his head to one side, looking into Amber's relaxed face, wondering just what might be going on behind those closed lids.

"I won't sleep with you!" she had declared so vehemently only a short time before. Not even two hours ago. "I won't. I'll never..."

And, "Never say never," he'd flung back, totally sure of himself—of her. "Never say never."

Dio! A rush of self-mocking laughter rocked his body and he shook his head in despair at his own foolishness.

So now what did he do?

Staring up at the ceiling, he ruefully reflected on what he had originally planned. How he had meant things to go from the moment he had learned about Amber's proposed marriage.

It had been Vito who had told him. His younger brother had come back from a business meeting in London in the foulest of moods but when questioned had refused to say exactly why. Instead, and obviously in an effort to distract Guido from his questions, he had announced that Rafe St Clair, a man they knew of only too well, was getting married.

He had had no idea of just how effective his diversionary tactics were.

Guido could still remember—still feel—the remaining embers of the world-rocking combination of shock, disbelief and white-hot rage that had shot through him when his brother had told him of the prospective bride.

'Her name's Amber Wellesley,' Vito had said. 'Apparently she lives in the same village. Her father was a friend of Rafe's father but he died before this girl was born.'

Sitting up slightly, Guido looked down into the shuttered face of the woman beside him. Did she know what it had done to him to find out that she was getting married? It had been bad enough when she had declared that she was walking out because he wasn't what she wanted—he wasn't good enough for her. She'd met someone else, someone with standing, with a lineage that matched her own.

Hellfire, it was a good thing that he had never, ever told her the truth about his own position, his own wealth. If he had she might have stayed—and he would never have been able to trust her reasoning.

No, he'd told her to go if that was the way she felt. He'd been so savagely furious that he'd damn nearly pushed her out of the door. But in the end, he'd been the one to walk out. At that moment he'd never wanted to see her again.

Besides, he'd been convinced that, given time to calm down, think things through, she'd come back to him. He'd never expected that she would actually go ahead and marry the man she'd left him for. And stopping that marriage had been the main thing on his mind when he'd come to England this time.

After that, he'd planned to take things slowly—check out how the land lay before he made any rash or foolish moves. He was definitely not going to let his libido rush him into things this time.

'Hah!'

Unable to stay still a moment longer, Guido started to swing his legs off the bed and froze in a moment of total shock.

He had been so out of control, so hot for Amber that he hadn't even taken his trousers off, for God's sake! What sort of man was he? What sort of an animal did she turn him into?

He had totally lost control—totally lost his mind. He didn't like what he became around Amber and that was the truth. What he became was a man who couldn't think clearly, couldn't act rationally. And as a man who had prided himself on doing both of those things, he was definitely knocked off balance as a result.

Swallowing down another curse, he sorted out his clothing in a rush, zipping up his trousers and pulling his belt tight with a viciousness that eloquently expressed the way he was feeling, before swinging away to the window and staring down at the hotel grounds, where the evening was now gathering in, turning the sunlight of the day into dusk.

'Guido?'

The voice—her voice—came from behind him. From the bed where he had thought—hoped—that she lay asleep. His unwary movements must have disturbed her and she was awake, well before he was ready to speak to her.

'Yes?'

He knew the single word was a bad-tempered snap but didn't turn to see the effect it had on her. Instead, he kept his back to her, stared determinedly out of the window even though his eyes were so unfocused that he couldn't see a thing in front of him.

'What do we do now?'

What do we do now!

She had asked him the question that had been in his mind ever since he'd come round from the frenzy of desire that had scrambled his brain. The question that he'd wanted more time to come up with an answer to.

'How the hell should I know?' he growled at the window, not ready to turn round and face her.

'What?'

His tone had been so low, so rough that she hadn't caught it.

'Guido, I wish you'd look…'

Her voice faded as he swung round, hands pushed deep into his trouser pockets, jaw clamped tight over the things that clamoured to be said—the things he wanted to say—didn't want to say. The things he had no idea how to say.

'I said, how the hell should I know?'

She was regretting asking him to look at her now, that much was obvious in the way that she flinched back against the pillows.

'I'm sorry…'

Conscience made him say it, but he knew that it came out far too abruptly and only sounded perfunctory. The truth was that he wished he hadn't turned round. That was another stupid mistake he'd made.

Just looking at her lying there on top of the rumpled covers of the bed had an effect that was practically sending his brain into meltdown. She was still wearing only the ridiculous corset thing, that and the suspender belt and stockings—and nothing else. Her hair was tumbled all around her face, her green eyes huger than ever in her pale face. Her lips looked swollen from the heat of his kisses and her beautiful breasts were bare and exposed, their rosy nipples still glowing from…

Porca miseria—no! He was not going to think about that! Couldn't think about it or he would lose what little grip he had on his self-control. Already, just looking at her, he felt the brutal clutch of lust between his legs, and in his concealing pockets his hands clenched into hard, tight fists to stop himself from pulling them out and using them to touch her—to arouse her again—to make her melt underneath him…

'No!'

His already savagely uneasy mood was made all the worse by the way that Amber was reacting. She was staring at him as if he had suddenly grown a pair of horns. And while her eyes held his, one slender hand was reaching down, trying to find an edge on the covers, to pull them back up around her, covering her nakedness.

'Oh, for God's sake!' he exploded. 'Isn't it a little late to go coy on me? It's not as if there's anything I haven't seen and touched—and more—already. And we are man and wife!'

'Not from any choice of mine!'

She was being deliberately provoking and he knew it. But he also had no idea of just how much truth was actually behind those words and, because he didn't know, it only added to his already unbalanced mood.

'That wasn't what you said the first time—then you couldn't get to the chapel fast enough. You couldn't wait. It was "Oh, Guido…can we do it soon? Can we do it here—now—as quickly as possible?" So I arranged a bloody wedding—I married you! And what do you do? You walk out on me as soon as you can to be with someone else.'

'I told you—I thought it was a fake marriage!'

She'd succeeded in pulling the sheet up now, wrapping it around her and tucking it tightly under her arms, over her breasts. But the truth was that it didn't make matters any easier. If anything, it made them worse.

He could still see the soft pink of her skin through the fine linen, the pout of her breasts was emphasised by the way she'd clamped her arms around herself underneath them, pushing them upwards, and the swell of her hips was an undulating curve to one side of the bed. Imagination combined with memory to act on the gnawing ache in his groin, driving him almost to distraction.

'And what the hell made you think that? Amber…' he insisted dangerously when she didn't answer and dropped her gaze to where her narrow fingers pleated the sheet in front of her over and over again. 'I asked you a question.'

Just when he thought she wouldn't answer and took a hasty step forward, almost on the edge of grabbing hold of her, shaking the response out of her, her chin came up and she met his searching gaze with unexpectedly cool defiance. Which was just as well as he knew that if he touched her now, for whatever reason, then he would never stop. It might begin in anger but as soon as he felt her skin underneath his hands then the mood would change. He would have to kiss her—and caress her—and then he wouldn't be able to stop.

'I heard you!' she declared, bringing his thoughts back to reality with a rush that jarred his brain painfully.

'You did what?'

'I heard you paying him—paying the man who'd arranged it all. I heard you thanking him for—for getting everything sorted out so fast.'

'Because that was how you wanted it!' Guido put in in exasperation. '"Can we get married tomorrow?"' he quoted her own words at her brutally. '"Just find a chapel here and—and do it."'

But it was obvious that Amber hadn't heard, or if she had then she was deliberately ignoring him.

'You—were grateful to him, you said…' she ploughed on, her face as stiff and cold as if it had been the face of a marble statue, the green eyes blank and opaque. 'Grateful to him for getting this farce of an event organised.'

Hearing his own words parroted back to him had an effect like being doused in icy water, freezing Guido instantly. His tongue wouldn't work, wouldn't let him say anything, particularly when she went on, recalling the conversation with devastating accuracy.

'You said you could only be thankful that this wasn't your real wedding as it was nothing like the one you'd imagined you would have if you ever were to be married. Not that you ever wanted to be married.'

'And that was the absolute truth. I never wanted to marry.'

It was only when the cold, controlled words fell into the silence that followed her words that Amber realised just how much—how desperately—she had been hoping for something else.

Had she really been stupid enough—weak enough—to dream that he might suddenly have recanted all he'd said to the man he was paying off that night in Las Vegas? Was she really that foolish?

A year ago, perhaps she might have been. For a few glorious, wonderfully happy days of her catastrophically brief marriage she'd been totally brainwashed, totally deceived by him. But then the things she had overheard had destroyed the foolish idyll she'd been living in.

She was supposed to have stayed in their hotel room, resting—resting after a particularly long and energetic afternoon of lovemaking—and waiting for him to come back from some meeting he'd had to go to, so that they could make love again. He'd told her that he would only be an hour, and when that hour had turned into two—and then almost another—she had started to worry. Dressing swiftly, she had made her way down into the hotel lobby—and there, hidden behind the large, ornate statue that filled the centre of the hallway, she had overheard Guido paying off the man he had hired to make their wedding look real.

'It was everything she thought it would be,' she'd heard him say. He'd even laughed—laughter that went straight through her heart like a brutal sword. 'But then, she knows no better. Wouldn't know a real wedding if she was at it.'

At the time she'd just reacted. She hadn't stopped to think, but had turned and run. By the time Guido had joined her upstairs, she had been almost packed—if flinging clothes haphazardly into a case, not caring which way they fell, could be called packing.

Her mind blanked over at the memory of the huge row that had resulted from that. So now she put all the hurt, all the bitterness of her memories as well as the new misery he'd just inflicted on her into her voice as she rounded on him.

'Oh, well, I'm glad that you do speak the truth sometimes! Because you certainly didn't when you married me. When you vowed to be with me for the rest of our lives together. It's a pity that it wasn't a fake marriage—then at least I'd really have been free of you when I left. I wouldn't be surprised if I could actually get an annulment if I could prove just how little you meant those vows, that you were lying—probably even perjuring yourself!'

'And how would you know?' Guido flung right back. 'All you cared about was getting a ring on your finger.'

He'd said the same thing on the day before she'd left him, Amber recalled bitterly. She hadn't been able to bring herself to tell him what she'd overheard, but she'd accused him of never having loved her, had tried every last desperate trick in the book to get him to say that he did.

'We never had a marriage!' she'd screamed at him from the depths of her pain. 'Not a real one.'

And, 'You can say that again,' he'd retaliated. 'What we have is most definitely not a real marriage—and we never had a real wedding. Not that you would know the difference.'

It was an accusation she couldn't deny. She had been so nervous at the thought of her wedding, unable to believe that she was actually going ahead with it, that she was really going to marry a man like Guido Corsentino and that he was going to marry her, that she hadn't even thought about the details, about the legalities. She had left all of that to Guido, let him handle everything, and stayed locked in her own little dream world of happiness, terrified that if she came out of it she might find it had all been a dream.

'I didn't want to stop and think about what I was doing! I just wanted it done and over with.'

'And why was that? Were you worried that Mamma might find out? Or was it just the idea that you were lowering yourself to marry a Sicilian peasant?'

'I never thought of you like that! I…'

She caught the foolish words back before they could escape her.

I only wanted to hurt you as you'd hurt me, was what she had been going to say, but she couldn't admit to that. He would see behind it to the truth. And the truth of how much she'd loved him was something she didn't want him to know. Because the wedding might have been real but Guido's reasons for marrying her after all had been as cold and calculated as she'd come to realise. He had only wanted to keep her in his bed and he had been prepared to go along with her need for a wedding in order to achieve that end. She might have been married to him but it had never been a marriage of love.

'No, you only realised how badly I compared to your English aristocrat when he came looking for you and you realised I would never be able to offer you the title of Lady anything.'

When had Guido moved?

She had been so intent on standing up to him, on showing him that he couldn't just walk all over her, that she hadn't noticed that he had taken several strides forward, coming so much closer to the bed. Now he towered over her, glaring down into her face, his eyes black as pitch and burning with molten anger.

But it wasn't the threat in them that dried her mouth, sending her throat into a spasm that killed any chance at all of speaking. It was something as equally primitive as fear but on the opposite end of the scale. It would have helped if he'd troubled to get dressed, but of course he hadn't. Guido had never given a damn about appearing naked, or semi-clothed, in front of her, his supreme self-confidence driving away any concern for modesty.

So that now, while she still huddled under the crumpled sheet, hiding away from him, he stood tall and proud, the broad expanse of his chest, the bronzed skin lightly hazed with jet-black hair, openly exposed. It was impossible not to remember how it had felt to be held against that chest, how the heat of his skin, the roughness of that hair, had rubbed against her sensitised nipples. Nipples that ached even now with the imprint of his caress, the longing for more.

Her fingers hungered to touch, to stroke over the smooth, satin skin, to feel the strength of muscle and bone. And between her legs heat pooled rapidly, tormenting her senses so that she had to shift uneasily under the light covering of fine white linen.

'No…'

It was a moan of protest at her own response that escaped her. She'd been burned that way already—burned twice, for God's sake—so what was she thinking of even being tempted again?

CHAPTER NINE

'No?' GUIDO questioned softly. Too softly.

Amber knew that voice of old. It was the one that he used when he was carefully reining in what he really wanted to say. When he was holding back the rage or the cynicism that in a weaker man would already have escaped, boiling over into dangerous fury.

'No? If it wasn't that, then what was it? You hadn't tired of me. I know it—you know it.'

To Amber's horror, he lowered himself onto the bed, coming to sit beside her, very close—too close.

Dangerously close.

She didn't know how to react. She wanted to run but she didn't dare. It would give too much away about the way she was feeling. She wanted to reach out and touch him, know the sensation of her fingertips on his skin, press her lips to him, taste him. But she didn't dare to do that either. And so she curled up in a tight little ball, twisting her legs away from him so that they wouldn't touch. She was afraid that she would feel the heat of him even through the linen of the sheet. That his touch might even burn her skin in spite of its protection.

'We never tired of each other, did we, Amber?'

'No...'

It was all that she could manage. She couldn't deny it after all. He had left her bed to go to that meeting. A bed in which they had just made mad, passionate love.

No! In her mind she corrected herself automatically.

A bed in which they had just had wild, fierce, abandoned sex. Sex that she had believed was making love but that he had seen as cold-blooded passion. A hunger for her that he would do anything to appease.

Even marry her.

'Why did you do it?'

'Why did I do what?'

His tone was disturbing, almost frighteningly gentle. Frightening because it sounded real. It sounded believable. And it was too tempting to believe in it. But believing that Guido did anything gently was a big mistake.

'Why did you marry me?'

'It was what you wanted. And I wanted you. If I could have had you any other way, I would have done it.'

Well, was that blunt enough for her? The bald, flat statement left no room for discussion or manoeuvre. He had seen something he had wanted and he had made the arrangements necessary to ensure that he got what he wanted. That was Guido Corsentino all over. What he wanted was what he got. No argument; no debate.

'I still want you.'

If it was possible, there was even less room for debate in that statement.

'So that answers your next question.'

'It does? And just what was my next question going to be?'

The sidelong glance that flashed at her from those deep, dark eyes warned against the note of flippancy that had crept into her tone. Don't challenge me, that look said. Don't even try!

'You don't even have to say it. It's written clear on your face—you want to know why I came after you, why you're here.'

'You came after me because you wanted to break up my marriage to Rafe,' Amber said slowly.

He might be right about the rest of the question that burned in her thoughts but she didn't want to risk opening up that particular can of worms. Because it inevitably led to another, more uncomfortable question—the one that went 'Why did you have sex with me?' Because there was no way on earth she could ask 'Why did you make love to me?'

'And because I still wanted you,' Guido put in, stilling her nervous tongue when she would have gone on. 'But it took the prospect of your marrying another man to make me see just how much.'

He was jealous! Amber didn't quite know why that should rock her world so violently, but it did. So much so that she actually put a hand out onto the surface of the bed to support herself when the room seemed to shudder around her. The movement made the sheet she had been holding to her gape widely at the front and she had to clutch at it frantically to keep it from falling. The resulting tug at her nerves made her voice sharp as she met his black, intent gaze.

'And is that supposed to flatter me?'

'I don't do flattery.'

The lift of Guido's broad shoulders shrugged off the question as unimportant.

'I would have come after you anyway—it's just that the need to stop your illegal marriage made me move rather faster than I'd planned.'

'You would have come after me?'

Amber couldn't believe what she was hearing. She had been so sure that she had slammed the door on that particular relationship—locked it and thrown away the key. She had never thought that he might actually come after her. But then of course she hadn't bargained on the fact that their marriage had actually been legal instead of the fake she had believed it to be.

'I was waiting for you to come to your senses.'

He sounded so confident, so totally sure of himself—and of her—that Amber could only gape stupidly, her eyes wide and glazed, her mouth falling slightly open.

'And now I suppose you think I should be thankful that you saved me from a bigamous marriage.'

Once again those broad shoulders lifted in a dismissive shrug. Amber tried not to notice how the movement flexed the muscles in his chest, defining the tightness of them, the narrow waist.

'You would never have been happy with St Clair.'

But that was too much. The arrogance of the way that he had moved in, taken over her life, turned it upside down, was more than she could bear.

'Did you even give me a chance to find out? Did it ever cross your mind that I might have wanted to be with Rafe?'

'Do you love him?'

The question came harshly, thrown into her face almost brutally so that she reared back away from it as if it had been an actual blow.

'Do you?'

'You asked me that once already; why ask it again?'

'Because you brought it up again. And isn't it a normal thing to ask of a bride on her wedding day? Wouldn't her family—her friends—want to know if she was in love with the man she was marrying?'

'You're neither my family, nor my friend.'

And the memory of just how little her mother had actually cared brought the sting of tears to her eyes, making her blink fiercely to drive them away. Under the covering of the sheet, the tightly boned basque was digging into her painfully and she wished she could take the time and space to adjust it. But with Guido still sitting so close, his eyes watching every movement, every expression like a hawk, she didn't dare even try.

'And you're never likely to be either.'

Oh, damn, damn, damn it! Just saying those words had made

the tears burn even more cruelly, and blinking so hard didn't seem to be working. Instead of holding them back it was making them spill out onto her cheeks, blurring her sight, soaking into her lashes.

'Don't worry, it's not your friend I want to be.' Was she imagining things or had there been the faintest of emphasis on that word 'friend'? 'So why don't you answer the question?'

'Why are you asking it?' Amber countered. 'Are you telling me that if I say I love him you'll let me go—set me free to be with him?'

The sudden hope in her eyes stabbed daggers at Guido, making him clench his hands furiously over the sheet, crushing it mercilessly. The temptation to gather it up and rip it from end to end to express the way he was feeling was a tormenting provocation in his thoughts, one he fought an ugly little battle with, only just managing to subdue it in time.

Just for a wild, crazy second, he almost wished that she was right. Wished that she could say she loved Rafe St Clair with all her heart, all her soul. At least that would get him off this appalling treadmill that he had been on ever since she'd left him. If he'd been able to believe that she truly loved any other man—even Rafe St Clair—if she could say that to his face and mean it, then he would have to let her go, he admitted to himself. He would have no option.

But of course she was never going to say any such thing.

So what was it that had brought tears to her eyes, spiking her long dark lashes and sparkling like diamonds against the blackness? The temptation to reach out and touch a finger to one of those sparkling drops ate at him inside so that he tightened his grip on the sheets again in order to resist it.

'You had your chance to say you loved him in the church,' he challenged her roughly. 'You didn't take it. You couldn't take it.'

Just for a moment she looked as if she was going to fight him on that. As if she was going to try and say he was wrong, even though they both knew before she started that she would never convince him.

Her green eyes flashed defiance, the warm pink lips even opened and she drew in a ragged breath…

Then let it out again in a sigh.

'No,' she admitted, low and soft. 'No, I'm not madly in love with Rafe.'

It was what he knew anyway. What he'd been wanting her to say, pushing her to admit. So what did he feel now that she had admitted it?

Nothing.

And that was the most disturbing thing. He had been thinking he would feel something—satisfaction at least. Satisfaction at the thought that she didn't care about someone who wasn't worthy of her love. Relief that he hadn't broken up a true match.

But instead he knew a strange emptiness where his feelings should be. And a cold, uncomfortable voice was whispering inside his head that of course she hadn't loved Rafe St Clair because when had Amber Wellesley—Amber Corsentino—ever loved anyone but herself?

With the thought of that name—that Amber Corsentino—came the sudden rush of realisation of an extra complication in this whole mess that had never entered his head until now.

D'accordo, no—it had entered his head, but he'd pushed it right out again. Other, more powerful feelings, at that moment more vital, more demanding feelings, had pushed it out again. And only now was he remembering it and looking at just what it really meant.

He was looking at the yawning gap between what he had planned to do, what had been in his mind as he made the journey from Siracusa to London, and from London to the village, and the church—and what had actually happened in that church. And here, in this hotel room.

'So now you know,' Amber was saying, bitterness darkening her tone, making her voice brittle. 'I suppose that condemns me totally in your eyes. Well, don't worry—you won't have to put up with me for long. We just need to ride these uncomfortable few days and then, hopefully, things will calm down.'

'You think they'll do that?' Guido questioned, looking into her face and seeing that realisation hadn't yet dawned there. She was still a couple of steps behind him on this. She had to be or she wouldn't be sitting there so calm and composed.

'Of course they will. It will be just a nine-day wonder …'

Something in his voice had caught on her nerves. The words faltered, faded from her tongue and she stared into his face in obvious uncertainty.

'You don't think they will?' she questioned sharply.

'We have to get out of here first.'

'Oh, I know that!' Amber actually sounded relieved. 'That won't be fun. But surely…'

Once more her voice faded as she watched his expression change. Guido was surprised that she couldn't read his thoughts in his face. He felt sure that every second of regret, of disbelief, of sheer blind fury at himself and the way he had handled this had communicated itself to her without any need for words.

Because he hadn't handled this in the way that he had meant to and because of that he had complicated things even more.

It had seemed so simple at the beginning. He was supposed to have walked into that church and stopped the wedding—then taken Amber away from there. Taken her somewhere where they could talk, where they could be alone together. Somewhere where they might have a hope in hell of sorting out this mess.

Somewhere where he could find out what she had really felt about him—if she felt anything. Where he could tell her the truth about Rafe St Clair and the bastard's real reasons for wanting to marry her.

Where he could see if they had anything that bound them

together other than that fierce, blazing passion that had put them in bed together from the start.

That passion was the thing that had caused all the trouble from the beginning. It had rushed them from a bed to the wedding chapel, into an ill-conceived and ill-thought-out wedding—and then back into bed again. And when they were in bed they didn't talk. They communicated in far more basic, far more fluent ways.

So this time he had vowed to himself that he would do this so very differently. He would not touch her, not even kiss her. He wouldn't risk a repeat of that fiery passion that had stopped them both thinking, stopped them ever getting to know each other, the first time. He would hold back, take things steady, turn the rush to the altar they'd had the first time into a steady, controlled voyage of discovery. That this time he would run his relationship with Amber with his mind and not with his hormones—and he'd see where that would take them.

And he'd failed completely.

He'd made a total, ruinous mess of the whole thing. He hadn't been able to keep his hands off her. He'd fallen into bed with her every bit as fast—faster—than he had done that first time. And so now here they were, both caught in the same cleft stick. Except that this time they were both painfully aware of the fact that this marriage was legal and binding and they couldn't get out of it and he was sure that Amber hadn't thought out the repercussions for herself.

'Dannazione!'

The viciousness of the curse brought him to his feet in a rush, slamming the fist of one hand into the palm of another as he paced his way around the room. The movement brought Amber's head round to stare at him, her eyes turning the colour of moss as they clouded with apprehension and confusion.

'What is it?'

With an effort Guido imposed a degree of control on himself, forced himself to swallow down the second outburst that almost escaped him. He even managed a smile, though his lips felt as if they were formed from marble and might split open on the movement.

'You're right,' he said, knowing he was avoiding the real issue, and suspecting that she realised that too. 'Getting out of here won't be fun. But we're going to have to venture out some time. So I suggest you get dressed and collect your bags and we'll head for the airport.'

'The airport?'

Amber's bright head went back, smoky green eyes narrowing in suspicion.

'Where exactly are we going?'

Where were they going? There was only one place he could think of where they would have the privacy they needed.

'Sicily. Siracusa in Sicily, if you want me to be exact.'

She didn't like the mockery of his tone. It showed in the quick frown that drew her brows together. Or was it that she was still assuming that he was the impoverished photographer he had claimed to be when they first met? In that case, she was very definitely heading for a shock.

It seemed that was what was in her mind because she studied him coolly and went on, 'Siracusa is where you live, I take it.'

'*Si*. Oh, don't look like that, *bellezza*. It really won't be quite as bad as you're expecting—in fact, it won't be what you're expecting at all. You see—'

'And what if I don't want to go to Sicily?' Amber cut into his attempt to explain the truth to her.

Oh, well, she'd see soon enough.

'I don't think you have a choice. We need somewhere we can stay and take stock and think about what our next move will be.'

'I don't need to think about it!'

Amber pushed herself off the bed, taking the sheet with her and wrapping it round her body like some sort of white linen toga.

'I don't want to go anywhere with you. And we don't have a next step to plan at all.'

'We don't?'

He laced the words with a note of warning, one that she seemed determined to ignore.

'No way! All I want is to wait for the furore that my aborted wedding caused to die down and then to organise a quickie divorce—and, believe me, it can't be quick enough.'

'No chance.'

Guido couldn't hold back the harsh bark of laughter that escaped him, drawing the full concentration of those green eyes to his face again.

'Why not?' she demanded.

'Why not?' Guido echoed cynically, drawling out the words deliberately. 'I should have thought that the answer to that was obvious to anyone. If you were hoping for a quickie divorce, *mia cara*, then I'm afraid you'd better think again. You see, what we did here, just now...' he nodded towards the bed, where the still rumpled bedclothes, the dented pillows, were blatant evidence of just what they'd been doing only a short time before '...will count as a renewal of our marriage.'

As he had expected, she looked appalled at the thought, her face losing all colour and one slender hand going up to her mouth to hold back the cry of horror that almost escaped it.

'But no one needs to know. If we don't tell anyone...'

'We don't need to tell anyone. They already know. Are you forgetting that we had an audience of hundreds—your former wedding guests—who were witnesses to the fact that we were shut in here for hours just after we declared to the world that our marriage was back on again? I'm damn sure that, if asked, any one of them would be happy to give evidence to that fact.

No, *carissima*, like it or not, I'm afraid we have to accept that in the eyes of the law we are very definitely man and wife again and this afternoon's pleasure is going to cost us dear in that it will have put the date of our permanent freedom from each other back by at least two years.'

CHAPTER TEN

IT REALLY won't be quite as bad as you're expecting—in fact, it won't be what you're expecting at all.

Guido's words replayed over and over inside Amber's head as she left the bedroom and walked out onto the balcony that overlooked the sea, stepping out of air-conditioned coolness and into the heat of a Sicilian afternoon. Her blue and green patterned voile dress swirled around her legs in a welcome breeze and the warmth of the sun beat down on her arms and shoulders exposed by the delicate shoe-string straps.

It won't be what you're expecting at all.

He could say that again—and again! This beautiful, luxurious, long, low-built villa perched right on the edge of a cliff, facing out towards the ocean, was the last thing she had been expecting when Guido had declared that he was taking her to his home.

Of course, by the time that they had left England for Sicily she had learned the truth—and discovered just how much Guido had not told her. But it had already been dawning on her before that. How could it not, when she had experienced the sort of first-class attention that had been lavished on her from the moment they left the hotel?

She should have thought of it earlier, too, she acknowledged grimly. The chauffeur-driven car that had taken them from the church to the hotel should have been the very first clue to anyone who was not completely stupid. But she had not been functioning on all cylinders at that moment. She hadn't been functioning at all. The shock and turmoil of her shattered wedding had devastated her thought processes, driving the ability to reason right out of her mind.

She hadn't felt much better when she'd left the security of the hotel bedroom, a place that had come to seem like a secure bolt-hole from all that had happened, and had ventured out into the world again. From the moment that the lift doors had opened to reveal that the huge marble-floored foyer was still crowded with Rafe's friends and family, the guests who had been invited to their wedding, she had known that Guido had been right. There was no way they could escape from here without anyone—without everyone—knowing.

The way that the crowd fell silent as they walked through the foyer, the buzz of conversation that started up behind them, following them like a wave rushing into the seashore, had all confirmed that he had been right. If the Press or anyone else wanted a story, there would be no shortage of people ready to step forward to give them one.

That thought had been enough to keep her quiet in the car, and at the first stage of their arrival at the airport, even though the questions were already surfacing in her mind. But it was her first sight of the plane that had brought her to a stunned halt, unable to believe the evidence of her own eyes.

'That is not any commercial plane!' she'd declared, turning furiously to Guido, who had only just managed to step to one side to avoid cannoning into her as she stopped dead right in his path. 'It's so small—it has to be a private jet—can't be anything else. So I think it's about time you did some explaining. Like who, for a start, does this thing belong to?'

'It's mine,' Guido told her. 'Well, mine and my brother's. It belongs to Corsentino Marine and Leisure—which Vito and I own.'

'Corsentino…' Amber shook her head in confusion as she struggled to take this in. 'I'm not going a single step further until you tell me exactly who you are and the truth about what you are.'

Amber flinched inwardly now as she remembered the nasty little public spat that had followed her declaration.

Guido had wanted to wait until they were on the plane, but she had dug her heels in and refused to move, causing him to hiss an explanation at her in a furious undertone. So intent were they on their own private conflict that it was only when a camera bulb had flashed over to their right, making them both start and blink, that they had become aware of the fact that they were still the centre of interest from the Press.

An interest she now understood much more than ever before.

Because Guido Corsentino was not just the photographer she had thought he was. The photographer who had stolen her heart and taken it away from her forever. He was Guido Corsentino of Corsentino Marine and Leisure. But it was only since she had arrived on the island that she had come to realise just how big that company was.

And with each new realisation of what Guido's life— Guido's real life—was like, it was as if she was taking another step backwards and further away from him. As if this man she now lived with, this man she was married to, became more of a stranger with each new discovery she made about him.

The truth was that she wasn't married to the man she'd thought she'd married. The man she'd told herself that she loved so desperately. But she didn't know if she loved this man. She didn't know him.

This was not the Guido Corsentino she had fallen so hopelessly, helplessly in love with. That man she had thought was a photographer, a man with a very basic income but huge amounts of charm, intelligence and endless sex appeal.

Nor yet was he the Guido Corsentino who had marched into the church a week ago today to break up her wedding and ruin her half-formed plans for the future. That Guido had at least had something of the old Guido about him, something that had reminded her of the man she had loved so much. Something that had brought her to make love with him again.

No, this Guido Corsentino was someone else again. A man of power and wealth, it seemed. A man who, along with his brother, ran a huge leisure corporation and speedboat-building business. This man was a stranger to her.

And a man who hadn't even tried to touch her since they'd arrived at his villa almost a week ago. Unexpectedly she'd been shown to this bedroom, and Guido had moved into another room, several doors down the corridor. She had spent her days lonely, and her nights alone.

Amber sighed, pushing back her hair from her face, and flexed shoulders that ached with the effort of holding them straight and not allowing them to slump. If she let them drop then she was sure that Guido would see it as a sign of weakness.

And weakness was something she was determined not to show him.

A sharp rap at the door of her room drew her attention back from her despondent thoughts and into the present. She was still debating whether or not to answer it when the door was pushed open and Guido strolled into the room.

'Did I say you could come in?'

Amber didn't care that she sounded aggressive and bad-tempered—she felt aggressive and bad-tempered. It was the only way that she could keep herself from falling into a pit of darkness and despair.

Was it really only a week since she had thought that she had her life all mapped out—that her future was planned, and she could finally move forward into it, putting the past behind her? Now it seemed that she had stepped back into that past and yet even that was a place she no longer recognised. Just as she no longer recognised Guido for the man she had thought him to be.

Even physically, he looked so very different. This man, so casually dressed in white polo shirt and blue denim jeans, was much more relaxed, comfortable, at ease in his own home, his own surroundings. The tan of his skin seemed darker, the jet-black hair gleamed more than ever in the brilliant light of the day, and the bronze eyes seemed to have caught a new heat and warmth from the sun so that they gleamed like molten metal, searing her skin at a glance.

He was more stunning, more devastatingly handsome than ever before, but this Guido was a man she didn't know.

'I did knock—and this is my home. Besides, you are my wife, and most married couples don't worry about modesty...'

'We're very definitely not like most married couples! In fact, I'd think that even saying we are man and wife is rather up for debate at the moment, isn't it?'

The dark frown that drew Guido's black brows together warned that he was fighting with his temper, but he managed to keep his voice smooth and even when he replied.

'And why is that, *mia cara*?' he asked, strolling across the room and coming to her side out on the balcony, where he lounged against the balustrade, indolently at his ease. 'I thought I had convinced you that our marriage was legal and above board.'

He was far too close for comfort and the way that the sun caught on the glossy black hair so that it gleamed in the light made her breath catch in her throat, drying her mouth. The clean, intensely male scent of his body seemed to fill the air around her, blending with some sharply citrus cologne in a way that tantalised her senses, making her blood start to race through her veins.

'But that was before you lied to me.'

She hated the way that her voice croaked betrayingly and reached for the glass of wine that she had brought out with her, praying he would take her reaction as simply the effects of the sun.

'I suspect that if anyone looked into that marriage certificate they might see you obtained it on false pretences!'

'And when, precisely, did I lie to you?'

Guido's tone was casual enough but those deep, dark eyes were fixed on her face, their scrutiny so intense that she shifted uncomfortably under it, feeling as if his gaze was actually searing her skin, branding her with its heat.

'When you told me you were a photographer.'

'No—'

One strong hand came up between them in a gesture that cut off her line of thought.

'I never lied to you. I simply said that I was in Las Vegas working as a photographer. Which I was. You assumed that that was all I was—in the same way that I assumed you were just the nanny you claimed to be.'

'I was just the nanny! I'd been working for an American family and the job had finished. I was having a holiday before I went home—I told you this!'

'But you didn't tell me you were the daughter of an English lord.'

Amber set the glass down on the stone balustrade with far less care than the fine crystal deserved and winced sharply as she heard the crash it made.

'The daughter,' she repeated, emphasising the word bitterly. 'And, according to English laws of inheritance, that means very little. Once my father died, the estate and the title all went to someone else—a male heir who could actually lay claim to them.'

'When did your father die?'

'I never knew him. He fell from his horse in a hunting accident and broke his neck months before I was born.'

'So you never had the title, or the land—or anything.'

'No. My mother did, of course. She loved all of that. In fact, it was the reason why she married my father.'

Something in Amber's tone caught on a nerve in Guido's thoughts and tugged hard. In spite of the sun on his back, the sound of the ocean lazily lapping at the seashore, he was suddenly back in the little English village church, seeing Amber sink down on the altar steps in near-hysteria, watching every member of the congregation get up and leave.

And he was watching Amber's mother, the one person he would have expected would stay to comfort, to support her daughter, but who did not. He was watching her turn and direct a look of supreme contempt and loathing right into his face— watching her twist on her heel and march straight down the aisle, after St Clair's family, without even sparing Amber a second glance. She walked out without a backward look, disgust, dark fury, and total rejection stamped into every arrogant line of her narrow-boned body.

'Have you contacted your mother since you came here?'

He had given her the freedom of the house, told her to use anything she wanted, whenever she wanted, and that had included the phone, the Internet… He strongly suspected that neither had even been touched.

The way that her face closed up, her eyes dulling and her mouth pulling tight, confirmed what he thought.

'No.'

The single syllable was low, bleakly despondent and so soft that if he hadn't seen her lips move he would barely have known that she'd spoken. But even as he strained to catch her response, he saw the way that she shook her head, sending the fall of chestnut hair flying in a soft halo around a suddenly pale face, and knew that he had heard right.

'No? Why not?'

'She wouldn't want to hear from me.'

'Are you sure?'

'She's my mother, Guido! I should know.'

It was said so coolly, with such total control, that for a moment he was taken off guard and believed in the impression she wanted to give him. But then he registered the tension in the words, a thickness in her tone that sounded like a struggle to hold back emotions she didn't want him to see. And when she walked away from him into the bedroom he couldn't miss the way that her spine was held unnaturally straight, her shoulders tight.

It was as if he was looking at her mother walking away from him down the aisle of the church. Except for one thing. There was something intensely vulnerable about the way that Amber held her slender body, something unnaturally taut in the fine bones, the long spine, something far too measured in the steps she took.

'Amber...'

She didn't turn when he spoke. Didn't give any indication that she'd heard. She just stopped beside the bed, still with her back to him, one hand going out to hold on to the edge of the carved wooden bed head, her fingers clenching tight.

'I'd like you to go now,' she said stiffly

'Not until we sort this out.'

'Sort what out?' Her tone was sharp and brittle and she still kept her head turned away, her attention apparently fixed fiercely on some spot on the far wall.

'Whatever's going through your head at this moment.'

'Then I'm afraid that you're doomed to disappointment. Because the only thing that's going through my head right now is that I wish you'd leave me alone. Like I said—'

'Look at me when you say that!'

The command cut harshly into what she had been saying, making her break off and stiffen again into silence.

'I said look at me when you say that.'

For a long moment he thought that she hadn't heard; or that she had, but was determined to ignore him. But then, at last, she drew in a deep, hissing sigh between her teeth and turned slowly, so slowly that it could only be a way of collecting herself, imposing control, before she came to face him.

'And I said I wish you'd leave me alone.'

Her eyes were clear and apparently dry, but there was a new

brilliance about them as if unshed tears had sheened their surface, and her hand was still fastened around the bed head.

'Not until you tell me what you did wrong.'

'What?'

That brought her gaze to him, staring at first and then narrowing sharply.

'What do you mean?'

Guido adjusted his position against the balustrade, leaning one elbow on the stone parapet and resting his head back against his upraised hand. The way that her eyes followed him, the new tension in her body, told him all that he needed to know.

Right now she looked like nothing so much as a startled deer, disturbed while grazing. One false move and she would turn and run, fleeing from him, and this moment would be lost— perhaps forever. And so he fought down the need to go to her, to hold her. He had touched on something important. And he did not intend to let go until he had found out exactly what.

'What did you do wrong to alienate your mother so much? What was your fault—in her eyes?'

He knew the moment she decided she was actually going to tell him and it came with those last three words. Up until then she had been stubbornly set against him, determined not to yield, determined to say nothing. It had been written all over her lovely, expressive face. But adding those extra words had made her pause. Made her rethink.

'Tell me,' he said softly.

Once more her breath hissed inwards unevenly and she made an odd little movement with her hand, brushing the backs of her fingers against her pale forehead as if wiping away an invisible cobweb.

'If you must know, I was born,' she said gruffly. 'And I was born a girl. That's what my mother can't forgive. My grandfather's estate could only be passed down to a male heir, and as my father died before I was born, the baby she was carrying was supposed to supply my mother with a title, the income—everything. But I was the wrong sex and, as a result, I got nothing—and neither did she. She's never adjusted—or forgiven me. As soon as I was old enough, I was bundled off to boarding-school while she set herself to catch a new husband. If she couldn't inherit a title, then she'd marry one...'

Her voice trailed off and she stared down at the polished wood of the floor, tracing a pattern on it with the toe of her pale leather sandal.

'She didn't succeed. She attracted plenty of men—had more affairs than I can actually remember. But none of them stayed. None of them wanted to marry her. And she had to watch my father's cousin living in luxury in Wharton Hall, with everything she wanted, everything a son would have brought her—everything I couldn't bring her because I was the wrong sex.'

Under the fall of his hair, Guido's hand clenched tight into a fist to express the barely controlled fury he was feeling at the way that Amber's mother had behaved. How could a woman be so selfish, so unfeeling—so damn greedy...? But he'd seen her. He'd seen the way she'd turned and walked out on her daughter.

An image of the way that Amber had looked then, huddled on the steps of the church altar, her bouquet limp in her hands, her head bent and her face hidden behind the veil, floated before his eyes.

'That was hardly your fault.'

Amber's smile was wan, a mere flashing on and off of a response, one that barely curved her lips before it was gone.

'I nearly did something right when it seemed that I was going to marry Rafe St Clair.'

For just a few short weeks she'd been the centre of her mother's world, Amber recalled. She knew that that, as well as the hurt of Guido's callous behaviour, had been behind her decision to accept Rafe's proposal of marriage.

He'd never seemed to notice her before, but now, after their chance meeting in Vegas, the meeting that had given her the excuse to leave, to get away from Guido and the marriage she had believed to be just a lie, he suddenly did. She had accepted his proposal on the rebound from the loss of her love for Guido and her mother's selfish pleasure in the engagement had at least brought a sort of peace to that difficult part of her life.

'And then I spoiled everything for you.'

Amber tried for another smile but failed, her lips twisting bitterly.

'The irony of it is,' she managed through the emotions that were clogging her throat, making it difficult to speak, 'that if my mother had only known about—about all this…' with a wave of her hand she indicated the luxurious room, encompassing in the single gesture the whole of what she now thought of as 'the other' Guido's life, the business and the money that she had never even guessed at when she had first met him '…she'd have welcomed you with open arms.'

'And you along with me?' Guido asked.

He straightened up and moved out of the sun, into the shade of the cool cream and white decorated bedroom.

'Very possibly.'

'Then why not tell her?'

'Because I've had enough of trying to win her love by what I can bring her rather than who I am. Because that moment she walked out on me on my—on the day I was supposed to marry Rafe left me in no doubt that I was never going to manage it. Anyone who cared would have stayed.'

She'd only told him half the truth, she knew. Less than half. Because the truth was that she could never use Guido in that way. And she could never try to win her mother's approval just for what he was, rather than who he was. She could never make his wealth so important a part of him when to her it was nothing. She had loved him when she had thought he had little money and…

'She should have stayed…'

Guido's words came to her only vaguely, muffled and distorted by the sudden roaring in her head, the racing of her blood through her veins that made her thoughts swim, ruined any chance she had of thinking clearly.

'She should have stayed…'

Anyone who cared would have stayed.

Guido had stayed.

When everyone else she knew had walked out of that church, when even her mother had abandoned her, lost and alone, Guido had stayed.

He had stayed with her, supported her, warned her about the paparazzi. He had protected her from the Press when she had tried to venture out, brought her back in, offered her a solution—and a way out.

Guido had been there for her.

So what did that mean?

From now on we're in this together, whether we like it or not.

She had loved him when she had thought he had little money and…

And nothing had changed.

She still loved him now. If anything she loved him more than ever before. And not just in the hungry, yearning sexual way she had felt in the hotel room on her 'wedding' day. This was deeper, stronger, more whole. It was a part of her, so rooted in the real essence of her that it could never be pulled out without destroying her completely.

It didn't matter who he was or how wealthy he was, or where he lived—all that mattered was that he was Guido. A man. And she loved that man.

The realisation was like a blow to her heart, making her reel. She couldn't see, couldn't breathe. Her hand went out blindly, seeking support, and she felt it taken in a warm, strong grip.

'Amber?'

Guido was looking at her with concern and she forced what

she hoped was a reassuring smile; one that she prayed gave away nothing more.

'Too much sun,' she said lightly. 'I'm not used to it.'

'I'll get you some water.'

There was a bottle and a glass on the bedside table, which meant that he had to turn his back on her to get to it, and, knowing she was unseen, she watched him as he picked up the bottle, unscrewed the top, poured…

Such ordinary actions but, done by him, by this man she loved, they seemed to take on a whole new significance. His hands were so strong and sure, the smooth skin tanned golden by the Italian sun. And underneath the bronzed skin the muscles in his forearms moved smoothly, easily, making her want to reach out and stroke her fingertips over their strength, feel the hardness of sinew and bone.

Or was it the width of his shoulders she longed to trace, finding the silk of his hair at his nape, tangling her hands in its softness? Against the white collar of his shirt, its colour seemed impossibly black, the starkest possible contrast, almost shocking in its dramatic effect. And the way that the worn denim jeans clung to his lean hips, smoothed down over long, powerful legs had more of an effect on her pulse rate, the heat in her own body, than any of the sun she had been exposed to during the day.

It was as if she had never seen him before, and yet at the same time it was as if he was the only man she had ever seen so that she couldn't stop looking, couldn't tear her eyes away from him but had to let them linger, absorbing every part of him as if he was some wonderful feast that had been set before someone who had been starving for months.

But then he turned and their eyes met and for a moment she just couldn't look away.

And she knew that the way she was feeling, the hunger that gnawed at her, the need, all must show in her eyes.

The hunger and need she could cope with. He knew about that. He'd understand that. He'd felt the same way. And she was sure that the same hunger burned there in the dark brown depths of his eyes, a strong, fiercely smouldering flame that she felt sure could devour her in a glance, blast her into a pile of shriveled-up ashes right where she stood.

But the love?

There was no way he would understand the love—or want it from her. Not after all that had happened between them.

And so she closed her eyes hastily, breaking the burning contact, needing to hide her vulnerability from him.

CHAPTER ELEVEN

'YOUR water...'

After the moment of intense awareness she had just experienced, Guido's words sounded so matter-of-fact, so down-to-earth that it almost hurt her to hear them. Had she imagined the heat in his eyes, then? Had it been there at all or had it been simply the reflection of her own feelings, mirrored and thrown back at her so that she had imagined what she most wanted to see?

'Thank you.'

Somehow she forced the words through a painfully dry throat that sounded raw enough to need every drop of liquid in the glass he held out to her to soothe it. But even taking the first sip proved almost impossible, the water at first refusing to slide past the knots that were closing off her breathing and only by gulping hard could she actually get it down. And as she gave a small gasp of relief when she did, she saw Guido's dark brows draw together in a quick, puzzled frown.

She had to say something, anything, to distract him. Anything to get his mind off her and on to something else before she gave things away completely, she told herself, scrabbling in the clouded muddle of her thoughts for a subject that would work.

'You never told me why you came in here,' she managed, struggling to ignore another flashing frown from those dark eyes that warned that he knew he was being deliberately diverted and he had little patience with her tactics.

At first she felt sure that he wasn't going to answer her but then he pushed back a lock of black hair that had fallen forward over his forehead, he folded his arms across his broad chest and followed her lead.

'My brother is coming for dinner. I thought you'd like to meet him.'

His brother.

Amber gulped down another mouthful of the water, thankful for its coolness on her burning throat. Since she had arrived here almost a week ago, she had seen no one but Guido and the near-silent, unobtrusive staff who waited on him, appearing to serve meals or clean the rooms. And that had been how she had wanted it. She had needed to hide away, come to terms with things. She hadn't even asked Guido what he had said in the statement he had promised the papers, assuming that he had stuck to the story they had agreed on—or, rather, the story he had said he would use and she had had no choice but to go along with.

But she knew that she couldn't hide away for ever and now the real world, in the shape of Guido's brother, Vito, was finally breaking into the private sanctuary she had made for herself.

'That depends on what you've said about me,' she said defensively.

'Well, naturally, I've told him that you're here, and that you're staying with me.'

'Staying with you as what?' Unease made her voice sharp. 'Have you told him I'm your wife?'

'Would you want me to?' Guido countered sharply. 'Do you want me to let Vito know that we're married?'

Did she?

Amber couldn't find an answer to that question, no matter how hard she tried. If she was pushed then her first, her instinctive reaction would be to say no, no way did she want Guido's brother to know who she was. She didn't want anyone else to know that she and Guido Corsentino were man and wife. Her life was already too complicated.

But even as she thought that, another opinion rushed into her head, pushing aside that first, instinctive reaction.

She was Guido's wife. In spite of all those months that she had spent bitterly regretting their marriage and wishing she'd never gone through with it, hating Guido for the deception—a deception she now knew that had never been—she was Guido's legal wife.

And she had just admitted to herself that she loved him.

Couldn't she take a chance on that? Work with it?

Was it possible that if she stayed, that if she spent the time with Guido that he had demanded, that if she lived with him, acted as his wife, made love with him, then it might just be possible that he might come to feel something for her?

He already did feel something if it was only the hot sexual passion that he had already showed her. Whatever else had died between them, that hadn't, as he'd made only too plain in the hotel room on the afternoon of her wedding day. OK, so he'd backed off since they'd come here to Sicily but there had to be some reason for that, surely? Perhaps he was letting her rest—pacing it—taking it steady... All of which sounded caring and considerate in a way that made her heart leap.

'Or would you prefer that to be our dark and dirty secret?'

She had hesitated too long and Guido's anger showed.

'It doesn't have to be that way!'

'No? Isn't that what you made me? Something you didn't want to remember? Something to sweep under the rug and so keep hidden from the world? Wasn't I your dark and dirty secret?'

'But not now! There's no need for that now—surely...'

The words dried, died, as she saw the look on his face, saw the cynical suspicion in his eyes, and something cold and nasty slid down her spine, making her shiver in apprehension.

'There's no need for that now,' Guido drawled sardonically, emphasising the last word with dark cynicism. 'And why is that, I wonder? What is it that makes me suddenly the sort of person that you don't want to hide away any more?'

The fact that I love you.

But she couldn't say that—not now. How could she say 'I love you' to the cold-eyed man who stood before her?

She knew what he meant, of course. She could almost read the thoughts that were going through his head, burning behind those golden-brown eyes. She only had to look around and see the beautiful villa where she was living, remember the private jet, the details she had learned of the way that the two Corsentino brothers had inherited a failing boat-building company and then built it up into the hugely successful business it was now. The design and production of a stunning new racing boat had increased both sales and reputation and had launched the company on the path to become the multimillion-pound Corsentino Marine and Leisure.

And of course Guido believed that that was why she no longer wanted to keep him hidden.

And so she hedged desperately, not daring to say out loud what was hidden in her heart.

'Well, it's rather pointless trying to hide anything when our names and faces were spread all over the tabloids back in England. And besides, what was it you said—never say never?'

That brought his dark eyes to hers in a rush, looking deep into hers, probing, searching...and she made herself hold that gaze as she put down the glass and took a single step towards him.

'What are you saying, Amber?' Guido questioned, and the huskiness of the words gave away the effect she was having on him—the effect that she wanted to have.

'I'm saying that, whether we like it or not, we're man and wife. Quite a lot of people know that already and—because of what happened in that hotel, we're not likely to get a quick and easy divorce any time soon, unless one of us gives just cause...'

The weak attempt at flippancy was failing, and she knew it from the way his dark brows drew together frowningly, so hastily she changed tack.

'We're together, and—well, why not take advantage of that fact…?'

Why didn't he say something, anything? Surely he understood what she was trying to say? So why did he show no reaction but just continued to regard her steadily from beneath hooded lids?

'Take advantage in what way?'

'You know what way!'

'You're going to have to show me. Come on, Amber,' he challenged. 'Don't make hints you're not prepared to follow through on.'

The deliberate provocation pushed Amber into taking another couple of steps forward so that she was right in front of him, almost up against him. She could smell the warm scent of his skin and hair, blending with the lemony tang of the shampoo he used. The soft sound of his breathing was the only other noise in the room apart from the lazy lap of the waves against the beach out beyond the window.

'What makes you think I'm not prepared to follow through, Guido?' Amber teased.

Her voice shook slightly as her nerves tightened. Was she really going to do this? *Could* she go through with it?

But then she touched him and immediately all thinking stopped.

The warmth of the skin on his cheek beneath her fingers made her heart lurch and judder. She wanted to touch all of him. It felt so right to her and yet there was no response from him. She could sense the tension in his muscles, feel them tighten under her touch.

'I don't make promises I don't intend to keep. And that's what I'm making, Guido—promises, not hints.'

This time she kissed him, her mouth where her fingers had been. And this was better—now the pressure of her lips against him had him drawing in his breath sharply and when the tip of her tongue slipped out to stroke a moist path along his jaw line he shuddered in uncontrollable response.

'Amber...'

Her name was thick and tough on his tongue and he couldn't stop himself from reaching for her, drawing her close. She came with him, just so far—and then she stopped, right in front of him.

This time she let her fingers walk up the front of his polo shirt, smoothing over the tight muscles of his chest, making them tighter, harder with each gentle sweep of her hand. She paused for a moment over his heart, intent on picking up the fast, heavy thud of his pulse. And when she caught it she looked up straight into his face, seeing there that heavy-lidded, hooded expression that was so deceptive.

She thought she knew what was happening now. He was going to let her play the game her way and take the lead while he took the role of the waiter, the watcher, the follower. The role of the one who was seduced rather than the seducer.

It was when her fingers stroked his skin in the open neck of his shirt that she felt the first tremors of defeat. The first agonising hints of a total meltdown of control. Somehow her thumb had found just the right spot at the base of his throat where his pulse raced and where the skin was so thin, and the blood so near the surface that she could sense each time it skipped, the way it throbbed.

'And I promise you,' Amber whispered, pressing closer now with the soft swell of her breasts crushed against his chest, cradling the aching swell of his erection in the curve of her pelvis, 'that I can give you the passion you need, the sensuality you crave.'

'*Dio mio*, Amber...'

The words escaped him on a moan and now, at last, he

reached for her, hauling her close. His hands closed over her narrow back, stroked up and down her spine, curving protectively about the delicate bones at the nape of her neck, going upwards to tangle and twist in the chestnut strands of her hair.

With several burnished locks coiled tight around his fingers he tugged hard, pulling her head back and holding her head just so that he could capture her mouth with his, plundering deep into the moist warmth to taste the very essence of her.

A couple of uneven, staggering steps brought them to the edge of the bed, their locked mouths not moving, tongues tangling, the yearning, demanding kiss not easing in the least. Guido's free hand found the curve of Amber's hips, palm smoothing over the soft swell of her buttocks, hard fingers digging into the cushion of flesh.

Her small, sighing wriggle of delight unbalanced them even further and they tumbled down onto the bed, Amber's length crushed beneath the hard strength of his powerful form. Her dress was caught up around her waist and the feel of his hot touch on the smooth, silken flesh of her inner thighs made her gasp in air as if she was drowning, going under for the third time.

'You see…' her lips were at his ear, the words a warm breath over the outer curve, swirling into his hair '…I know what it was like between us; what it can be like again…'

She tried to kiss him again but suddenly something had changed. Changed utterly. Changed terribly.

'No!'

She barely registered the word through the roaring inside her head. But then with a savagery that tore at her senses he wrenched himself away from Amber's arms, from her kisses. Jackknifing off the bed with a force that catapulted him more than halfway across the room, almost out the door before he realised it, he raked both hands through his hair as he turned a look of such fury, such dark disdain on her that she shrank back on the bed, her hair flung wildly on the pillow, her mouth forming a shaken, 'Oh…'

'No—damn you! I'm not getting caught that way…'

'C-caught…'

Her legs were splayed wide, the blue and green dress bundled up around her waist, exposing the white softness of her thighs. But she didn't have the strength to move or care. Even the frustrated screams of her aroused body were drowned out by the thunder of shock and confusion that pounded inside her head.

'Yes, caught! We don't go down that path, ever again! Never!'

And before she could say another word or make a move to hold him back, he swung on his heel and headed out the door, letting it slam hard behind him like a furious and final full stop to all that had gone before.

Amber lay there, struggling for calm, her breath coming in raw, uneven pants, her thoughts just a whirl of pain.

What had happened? What *had* happened? And, even more important, *why* had this happened?

She had been so sure that that was what Guido wanted. She had known it was what she wanted…

But then realisation hit her with the force of an explosion right in her face, blasting her heart into tiny, irreparable pieces.

In her memory she was suddenly back in the church on the day of her wedding to Rafe. Standing in the aisle and listening to herself declare to Guido's face that she would never sleep with him. Never.

And, 'You, *carissima*, are a liar,' Guido had told her softly. 'Your words are a lie—your protestation too. You lie even to yourself—and you don't do it terribly well. I shall enjoy proving your words to be untrue, even if it takes me some time. One day you will come to me, begging me to forget you ever said such things—and I…I will be waiting.'

In that moment she had thought that when he said that he meant that he would have his revenge on her by taking what she offered when she had broken down and admitted that she couldn't resist him.

Now she realised that he had meant something much, much worse. That the revenge he had aimed for had been far crueller than she had ever anticipated.

One day you will come to me, begging me to forget you ever said such things...

And she'd begged all right. Maybe not with her words, but she'd begged with her actions, with her body. With the body she'd offered to him on a plate. Putting herself into his hands. His to do with as he pleased. The only gift she had thought that he wanted from her.

And he had spurned that gift.

He had let her beg. He had even, for a while, cold-bloodedly encouraged her with his kisses, his caresses.

And then, just when she had thought that they could at least have this...that this was one way they could communicate together, something that bound them together instead of driving them apart...

Then he had thrown her gift, and her heart, right in her face and walked out, making it bitterly plain that there was nothing he wanted from her any more.

CHAPTER TWELVE

'You must be Amber…'

Vito Corsentino was so like his brother that it made Amber's head reel. For all that there was only eighteen months between them, Vito was so very similar to Guido that they might have been twins.

In fact, the likeness was so pronounced that for a moment, when she had first walked into the downstairs lounge and seen the tall, dark-haired, strongly built man standing by the fire-place, she had thought that he was Guido.

At least until he had smiled. And then she had known without a doubt that he wasn't the man she loved but his younger brother.

Guido would never have smiled at her in that way. He'd never done so in all the time she'd known him and he most definitely wouldn't have smiled at her at all tonight.

Tonight, she would be lucky if he even spoke to her.

She hadn't seen him since the moment that he'd stormed out of her room, leaving her shattered and gasping in shock from the sudden ferocity of his withdrawal, the violence with which he'd slammed out of the room. She still didn't know what had happened to change his mood, in an instant, it seemed, from ardent lover to savage rejection and she hadn't had a chance to ask him anything about it.

He had kept his distance from her for what had remained of the afternoon, and the only communication she had had with him had been in the form of a note that had been delivered to her by one of his members of staff.

If the handwriting on it was anything to go by, the letter had been written in much the same sort of mood as the one in which he had left her room. The black, slashing scrawl had simply read:

My brother will be here for dinner at 8. I expect to see you then. Wear something appropriate.

So what, Amber couldn't help wondering, was 'appropriate' under these circumstances?

Was she meeting Vito as his brother's wife? Or simply as the latest lover in residence? And what would Guido consider appropriate for any one of those?

In the end she'd decided to go for the sort of sophistication that at least gave her morale a boost as she surveyed her image in the mirror. The lacy black crochet dress clung to her like a second skin and it was designed to look as if she wasn't wearing anything underneath it when in fact she was totally covered by the flesh-coloured slip lining. It was a dress she had bought in a rush of rebellion when shopping for clothes for her honeymoon. As she knew Rafe and his family's conservative standards, everything else she had bought had been perfectly modest—even staid. But then she had seen this dress on a display in a boutique window and had been unable to resist it. Especially when she had seen how it fitted her.

Now it gave her spirits a much-needed lift as she had pinned her hair up in an elegant coil at the back of her head, wearing long silver drop earrings as her only jewellery. A touch of mascara and a little lip gloss were all she needed to add to the light tan her skin had acquired in the week she'd been in Sicily and she felt ready to face what was coming.

Ready to do battle if she needed to.

All the same, it had taken every ounce of nerve she possessed to step into the room and she had spent a couple of moments outside the door drawing on all her courage and inhaling several long, deep breaths that she hoped would calm the way her heart was fluttering, stop her stomach from tying itself into tight, painful knots. Now here she was, with Vito, and there was no sign of the other dark, handsome man she so longed and yet so dreaded to see.

'Yes, I'm Amber...'

It wasn't just uncertainty that made her voice quaver as she took the hand that Vito held out to her. It was the impact of his looks—so, so like his brother's and yet so very different. They had the same height and build, the same strong facial structure, the same jet-black hair. But where Guido's eyes were that burning, molten bronze, Vito's were more of the darkest grey, almost black. Vito's soft blue shirt and beautifully tailored grey silk suit were more formal than anything she had ever seen Guido wearing, even on their wedding day, but it was that certain indefinable quality about him that set them apart from each other.

And the difference, of course, was that she loved Guido, where to her, at least, Vito was simply an astoundingly good-looking man.

'Guido said that I should come and meet his new girlfriend. Can I get you a drink?'

'Mmm—yes, please; white wine...'

Amber could only be grateful that Vito was turning away from her to pour her drink as she spoke. At least his diverted attention gave her a couple of much-needed moments to pull herself together. He didn't know it, of course, but if Guido's brother had actually thrown his own drink right in her face, leaving her dripping and gasping, it couldn't have had a more shocking effect on her.

His new girlfriend.

So that was how Guido had described her to his brother when he had invited him here. Come and meet my new girlfriend. She could almost hear him saying it, with just the right casual sort of intonation to imply that this girl was nothing special, someone who looked good on his arm, someone to pass the days—and the nights—with, but in the end not someone who would be around for long.

Unlike a wife.

So there she had it—the answer to the question that Guido had avoided giving her upstairs earlier that afternoon.

'Do you want me to let Vito know that we're married?' he had demanded harshly. 'Or would you prefer that to be our dark and dirty secret?'

She hadn't been able to answer him—except in a way without words. But he, it seemed, had rejected that attempt at communicating and turned instead to his own way of making his opinion plain. And if he had flung the words right in her face, his face ablaze with rejection and scorn, then he couldn't have made his meaning any clearer.

She was his 'girlfriend', not his wife. And it seemed their marriage was to remain the 'dark and dirty secret' that Guido had kept from his brother ever since the day they had made their vows.

The stab of pain was brutal in its cruelty, making bitter tears burn at the backs of her eyes until she had to blink ferociously to keep them from spilling out, tumbling down her cheeks. The glass of wine that Vito offered her shook in her hand as she took it from him and she took an unwisely large gulp of the cold, crisp liquid in order to try and get a grip back on herself.

'So where did you two meet?'

'In England...'

It was Guido who answered for her when she couldn't think of what might be the best thing to say. He had appeared in the doorway while Amber's back was turned and she had no idea quite how long he had been standing there, watching them, before he drew attention to his presence by speaking.

'Amber was to have been the bride at Rafe St Clair's wedding.'

'You're that Amber!'

Vito's astonishment was sharp enough to distract him from anything else so that he didn't notice the sudden stiffening of Amber's spine as Guido strolled into the room or the way that the kiss his brother dropped on her cheek was merely a coldly casual peck, with no real affection or warmth in it at all.

Amber noticed though. Noticed and felt the withdrawal, the distance that Guido was deliberately putting between them after the scene in the bedroom earlier. He was making it plain that, whatever he might have told his brother, they were really not together at all. Certainly not the lovers that Vito might believe them to be.

And not the man and wife that they had been once.

Amber's head was spinning in a mixture of pain and uncertainty. She had no idea what to think. No idea how to react. She tried a smile and felt her lips too tight and stiff to manage anything real. There would be nothing in her eyes either; she couldn't hide the unease that gripped her.

'Then you've had a lucky escape.'

'We'll leave that subject for now,' Guido growled.

He gave his brother a warning glance before Vito embarked on anything that would be best left unsaid. He should have told Vito that the topic of the wedding was forbidden territory. There were too many complications there, too much that still hadn't been brought out into the open.

He'd spoken too roughly, unable to control his tone, and the look that Vito shot back at him told him that he was in danger of giving himself away. He had to crush down the savage feelings that had gnawed at him from the moment that he had reached the doorway and seen Amber in the room.

At first he had thought that she was actually naked under the black lace effect of the dress she wore and the instant increase in his heart rate, the spike in his blood pressure had been savage as a result.

The fact that she actually had some sort of lining to the dress came as a belated realisation, but too late to do anything to calm his already jagged mood. Frustration still raged inside him like a fire, searing over nerves stretched way too tight by the unappeased lust that he'd been trying to deny ever since this afternoon.

Trying to deny without any hope of success. He had tried to work but his mind had been crowded with erotic thoughts, his concentration shot. He hadn't even dared to go to her room or speak to her to tell her the arrangements for tonight but had sent a note with one of his staff, asking her to be ready for dinner. He was pretty sure that any handwriting expert could have taken one look at the scrawled message, with the vicious pressure of his pen revealing far too much about his mood for comfort, and been able to analyse just the sort of irritation that was gnawing away at him inside, preventing him from thinking straight or acting in any way normally.

So to see Amber chatting easily to his brother, smiling at Vito while wearing the sort of dress that was guaranteed to send any man's pulse rate soaring, was almost more than he could take. He could only cope with the feelings it created in him by imposing a ruthless control on every sense, every movement, every thought. Even the kiss of greeting he had felt obliged to deliver had been the coldest of pecks, the briefest possible touch and then away again, his body held stiffly distant from her because any connection was sure to send his already smouldering body into raging flames that he had no hope of controlling.

Somehow he got through the evening. He managed to make conversation of a sort, if only by discussing company business with Vito, knowing that he was deliberately blocking Amber out of the dialogue by talking of things she knew nothing about. And when Vito tried to make the discussion more general he could only manage to follow part of the way. Then the sight of Amber sitting opposite him at the table, with her eyes wide and bright, her slender neck exposed by the elegant hairstyle, the scooped neck of her dress revealing the delicate bones of her shoulders, the soft golden tone of her skin, the sweet swell of her breasts, had destroyed his ability to think. He had resorted to just watching her, giving up any attempt at following the conversation, simply adding a yes here, a no there and praying that his responses fitted.

He had determined that he wouldn't sleep with Amber until he knew just what she felt but now he was forced to question the wisdom of his decision. If sex confused and complicated the issue, then no sex scrambled his brain completely. He couldn't think straight and the truth was that he was no closer to understanding the way that Amber's mind worked—if anything, he was further away from it than he had ever been.

'More wine, Guido?'

Vito's voice broke in on his brooding thoughts, forcing him back to the present in a rush.

'I'm fine…'

'But your glass is empty.'

Was it?

Glancing down at the fine crystal that was still loosely in his hand, Guido was stunned to see that where he expected it to be at least half full of the rich, ruby wine they had been drinking, it was actually completely empty.

And he didn't have any memory of drinking a single drop.

'Do you have the smallest idea what we've been talking about?' his brother demanded, an edge of exasperated amusement in his tone.

'Etna!' Guido snapped. 'What does any visitor to Sicily talk about but the volcano?'

The amusement in Vito's eyes grew. 'We finished with the volcano ten minutes ago. You've been in dreamland since then.'

Sighing, he set down the bottle of wine he'd been offering, draining the little that remained in his own glass.

'I get the impression that I am definitely *de trop*,' he murmured wryly. 'Time I was leaving.'

'Not on my account!'

Try as he might, Guido couldn't inject any genuine reluctance into his voice and it was obvious from the look that Vito slanted him that he was not at all convinced.

'I think it would be…tactful…if I left you two alone.'

'There's really no need.'

Amber sounded as uncomfortable as Guido did. So was the thought of being left alone with him so repugnant to her? The truth was that she had barely met his eyes once during the whole evening and he was sure that she had hardly touched her meal but had spent most of the time simply moving it about her plate in a pretence of being interested in it.

So was she regretting her earlier attempt at seduction? And if so, why had she done it? Because she really wanted him or because now that she had found out that he was a very wealthy man—far more wealthy, in fact, than the blue-blooded St Clairs—she had decided to give their marriage another try? From the beginning, she had been determined that they wouldn't sleep together—this afternoon she had been equally determined that they should. He had no way of telling the reasons for her decision and just the suspicion was eating him up inside.

'It's obvious that you two have things to talk about.'

Amber had pushed back her chair and stood up, tossing her napkin down onto the table.

'I'm tired and I—I have a headache.' She rubbed her temples as if to confirm the fact and, watching her, Guido admitted that she looked pale enough to justify her claim.

'So I suggest you stay and talk to your brother, Vito. It was nice meeting you. Goodnight...'

The tiniest flick of a glance in his direction and away again just about included Guido in her farewell and then she was heading for the door. With a rush of movement Guido forced himself to his feet, reaching the door just before she did and grabbing hold of the handle to open it for her.

'We need to talk,' he muttered in a low, urgent undertone, pitched so that it wouldn't reach his brother's ears.

The green eyes that lifted to his face were blank, opaque, totally distant. It seemed impossible that they could belong to the same ardent, passionate woman he had held in his arms only a couple of hours before.

'I think not,' she said coolly, her tone freezing him like the glance from those eyes. 'I really am very tired.'

And when she moved past him she held her body so stiffly taut that in spite of the constricted space it was impossible for them to touch, even to brush against each other just for a second.

'*Buona notte,*' Guido managed distractedly, unable to stop himself from watching the movement of her hips, the sexy sway of her buttocks as she walked away down the hall and started to mount the stairs.

Just for a second he was tempted to go after her, to catch hold of her arm, pull her to a halt, force her to listen...

But then he heard the soft sound of laughter behind him and, realising that he had totally forgotten his brother's presence, turned sharply to see Vito picking up the wine bottle again and refilling his glass, shaking his head as he did so.

'Oh, *mio fratello,*' he said, amusement still threading through the words. 'You really have got it bad. I don't think I've seen you like this since the time you came back from America when some woman there had broken your heart.'

'America is in the past!' Guido snapped and knew immediately that his reaction was a mistake. His tone of voice, his whole attitude, had alerted Vito to something he didn't want his brother to know.

'America might be in the past but this Amber definitely isn't,' he commented, taking a leisurely sip from the wine in his glass.

Suddenly his dark gaze sharpened in a way that Guido found particularly discomfiting.

'They're the same woman, aren't they?'

But Guido wouldn't let him finish.

'Enough! When you tell me about your love life, little brother, then you'll have the right to discuss mine.'

'So you admit it is your love life we're discussing,' Vito teased, waving the wine bottle in the direction of Guido's glass.

'I'm admitting nothing.'

Guido allowed him to refill his drink, if only in the hope of distracting his brother from the direction his thoughts were taking. Because the truth was that he couldn't answer him.

Vito had used the word that he knew he had been avoiding from the start. From the moment in which he had decided that he had to stop the St Clair wedding—and precisely how he was going to stop it.

In that moment he had told himself that he was looking for revenge for the way that Amber had treated him. *D'accordo*, he'd admit it to himself at least—revenge for the way she'd broken his heart. He'd fallen wildly, crazily in love with Amber in the first second he'd seen her in a hotel foyer in Las Vegas, and from that moment he had known he would do anything to get her into his bed—and then to get her to stay there. Especially when it had seemed that she was about to rush away again. Back to London at her mother's command.

Even go along with her mad idea for a rushed and cheaply tacky wedding that was nothing like the way he wanted to marry his bride, the woman he wanted to be with for the rest of his life. He could go through with this for now. Later, when he knew she was truly his, he would make the arrangements for the real ceremony of blessing, one that showed her how much she really mattered to him.

He had never got the chance. Their marriage had barely lasted a month before Amber had walked out with Rafe St Clair, leaving behind the vicious note that had told him she had found someone who suited her so much better. Someone who could give her the things he couldn't.

He'd hated her then. And he would have sworn that he still hated her when he'd walked into the church, bent on breaking up her second wedding. But something had changed in the moment that he'd seen her and he'd never been able to get back that fierce, powerful conviction ever again.

'So you only went to England to destroy that wedding because of the groom, hmm?'

Vito was clearly determined not to be distracted and his comments were more perceptive than Guido liked.

'Getting revenge on St Clair was certainly the main thing on my mind,' he lied brazenly, not caring if his brother was convinced or not. 'We've been waiting a long time for that satisfaction and I wasn't going to let the chance go.'

Reaching for his glass, he took a long swallow of the wine and as he did so a memory surfaced which gave him the perfect way of diverting Vito's attention again.

'Which reminds me…I had a rather strange experience at that wedding. When I first appeared, a woman in the congregation fainted and had to be carried out.'

'Your overwhelming sex appeal, obviously,' Vito drawled, grinning. 'You always did have that effect on women.'

'Well, in this case, I suspect it was more your overwhelming sex appeal,' Guido told him. 'Because later, at the hotel where the reception was being held, I met her again in one of the corridors. She went white as a sheet then too. But it was what she said—Vito, she used your name. She thought I was you.'

He had Vito's full attention now. His wine glass ignored, his brother was leaning forward in his seat, his hands clenched together on the white linen tablecloth. And his deep grey eyes were fixed on Guido's face.

'What was she like?' he demanded sharply. 'Did you get her name?'

'Short blonde hair—blue eyes—about so tall…'

He held his hand to where the blonde's head had come at his shoulder.

'I didn't get a name.'

'Emily…' another voice chimed in. The last voice he had been expecting.

Amber's voice.

'That's Emily you're talking about. Emily Lawton.'

She was standing in the doorway. She had taken the pins out of her hair and let it fall loose around her shoulders, but otherwise she was still dressed exactly as she had been when she'd left the table. The stunning lacy black dress still clung to every inch of her curves, still revealed the long, slender legs in the ridiculously high-heeled shoes. But this time, for once, that was the last thing on Guido's mind.

When had she appeared? was the one question that came straight into his mind, making his thoughts reel as he traced the conversation with Vito back, fighting to recall exactly what they had said and in what order.

Just when had Amber come back into the hall, arrived in the doorway?

How long had she been standing there, and, more importantly, just how much had she heard?

CHAPTER THIRTEEN

AMBER wished that she had never decided to come back down to the dining room, or that, having come back, she had never opened her mouth to speak.

It would have been so much better—safer and wiser—if she had simply kept quiet and crept away again. Guido and Vito had been so intent on their conversation that they wouldn't even have noticed she was there. But then she'd heard Guido talk about the blonde woman who had fainted in the church on her wedding day and before she'd been able to stop herself, the word 'Emily' had been out of her mouth before she had even realised it was open.

So now both Guido and Vito were looking straight at her. Two pairs of dark eyes were fixed on her face, each of them frowning slightly but in two very different ways.

If she'd really gone—or if she'd never come back down—then she would never have heard Guido declare exactly why he'd gone to England. And now that she'd heard, she couldn't un-hear it or wish that it wasn't true.

She had been deluding herself all along. She'd actually thought that *she* had been important in all this. That *she* had been the focus of Guido's actions. And that had given her a false sense of security—a feeling that she mattered. Even if it was because Guido hated her, then at least that was something he *felt* for her and something she could try to change or at least work from.

But—'Getting revenge on St Clair was certainly the main thing on my mind,' Guido had said, making it plain that he hadn't even thought of her at all. And it was shocking just how much that hurt. The words had ripped through her, tearing her heart to shreds with the thought that she had only been a means for exacting revenge on someone he truly hated.

'I—came to ask if you had anything for this headache...' she managed now because something had to be said, and obviously neither Guido nor his brother was going to be the one to say it. 'Otherwise I don't think I'm going to be able to sleep.'

She wished now that she'd gone with her first plan, which had been to get away and hide in her room and not come out again until she absolutely had to. Just sitting with Guido and watching him scowl his way through the evening had been ordeal enough and so she had snatched at the escape offered her by the fact that Guido and his brother clearly had things they needed to talk about. The revenge they had plotted on the St Clairs obviously being one topic.

But she had only got a little way up the stairs before she had been forced to admit that unless she took something for it then her headache was going to keep her awake long into the night. And lying awake, with pain pounding at her temples, so that she would inevitably be forced to keep going back over the events of the afternoon, the discomfort and stress of this meal, was something she dreaded.

And so she had come back down.

And oh, how she wished that she hadn't.

'I'll get you something...'

Guido couldn't have made it plainer that he too wished she hadn't come back and the speed with which he left the room in search of the tablets was the last straw. If it hadn't been for Vito's presence, Amber suspected that she would have sunk into a chair, put her head down on the table and howled out all the misery that was in her heart.

But even Vito didn't appear to notice her very much.

'Emily Lawton...' he repeated, and he sounded stunned.

'Yes. Her husband was a friend of Rafe's, but he died a couple of months ago. You didn't know she was married?' she asked as she saw his start of obvious shock.

'I didn't know he was dead. Amber...'

For a moment Vito obviously considered, then he inclined his handsome head in a sharp, swift nod of acquiescence.

'Do you have an address?'

He reached into his jacket pocket and pulled out a small notepad and pen, barely waiting for her to scribble down what he needed before he had snatched it back again.

'Tell Guido I'll be in touch.'

He was heading towards the door as he spoke but, almost out into the hallway, he paused, swung back just for a moment.

'And give that bullheaded brother of mine a message from me. Tell him that if he lets you go a second time, then he's even more of a fool than I thought.'

'But...' Amber began but Vito had gone before she could get any more words out.

'Let you go?'

This time the words came from behind her, making her spin round in shock. Guido had come back in the room, obviously just in time to hear his brother's last comment, but he was clearly only shrugging it off in a mood of dark scorn.

'My brother doesn't know what he's talking about. As I recall, I had no choice but to let you go. By the time I got back to the room you had packed your bags and moved out. Here...'

He tossed a silver-foil-wrapped strip of tablets down onto the table and placed a glass of water beside them.

'For your headache.'

'Thanks.'

Amber said it automatically but she didn't make a move to pick up the painkillers. Unexpectedly, the tension in her head seemed to be easing, which was strange because the look on Guido's face, the dark flames that burned in his eyes, seemed more the sort of thing that would increase the stress rather than reduce it. But instead she was getting a feeling that was like the sensations she experienced on hearing the first distant rumble of thunder after a day in which the atmospheric pressure had built up and up to an unbearable point.

Knowing that the storm was actually about to break brought such a rush of relief that it was better than any medication. Of course, she still had the tempest itself to come, and that might be devastating, but that was better than waiting and not knowing.

'I left because I—I didn't think you were coming back.'

'Not coming back? Of course I was coming back! You were my wife. Not that that was what you wanted.'

Amber winced inwardly as she remembered the appalling row they had had. A row in which she had told him that she didn't believe in their marriage—that she was thankful it wasn't real because that meant she didn't have to stay around and face the mistake she'd made.

'I thought...'

'I know what you thought.'

He removed his jacket, tossed it onto a chair, tugged his tie loose at his throat and unfastened the top button of the white shirt beneath it. The change in his appearance was more than just in the way he was dressed. Suddenly, from looking every inch the sleek, sophisticated, wealthy businessman he had been all evening—Guido Corsentino of Corsentino Marine and Leisure—he had gone back to being someone much more relaxed, more human somehow. Amber had to swallow hard as a knot closed up her throat and something tore at her heart with the realisation that now he looked much more like the Guido Corsentino she had first met in Las Vegas.

'You thought that I just married you to get you into my bed. Well, maybe you're right. I would have done anything to keep you there, that's for sure. But you weren't prepared to listen to reason—to realise that the marriage *was* legal, no matter what you thought.'

'You didn't stay around to reason!'

Amber wasn't prepared to take all the blame. She knew she'd made mistakes, but so had he.

'As I recall, you walked out…'

'I walked out to give us both time to calm down. So that you might be prepared to listen when I got back…'

Guido raked both his hands roughly through his hair, ruffling its jet-black smoothness.

'I walked for miles.'

He'd only planned to take just enough time to calm himself down, take the edge off the rage that had built inside him at the things Amber had said. The way that she had flung in his face that she was actually glad that their marriage wasn't real, because she had known that it was a mistake from very the first morning, from the moment when she'd woken up beside him. But going over and over it inside his head had made matters so much worse, adding fuel to the flames of his anger. Going back in that mood would have only made matters worse.

And so he'd stayed. He'd stayed out what he believed was long enough for Amber to have fallen asleep so that he could make his way back into the room in silence and leave any further confrontation until the morning.

What he hadn't been expecting was to get back to an empty room, all Amber's clothes removed from the wardrobes, her case gone—and that note lying on the pillow on his side of the bed.

When he'd seen that, it had been as if he'd been stabbed right in the heart. She hadn't pulled any punches.

'Are you saying that you waited around? That you actually wanted to give me all that stuff that was in the letter right to my face? That you would have faced me out—confronted me with Rafe St Clair, whose blue blood and aristocratic lineage made him so much more of a prospect than—?'

'Than a not very successful photographer?' Amber cut in. 'But you weren't that really, were you? You were never just the photographer you claimed to be.'

'I was then.'

Seeing her frown, Guido pushed a hand through his hair again and reached for a chair, pulling it out from the table. With a wave of his hand he indicated that Amber should seat herself in it.

'If we are actually going to talk then we might as well make ourselves comfortable.'

He waited as she sat down then followed suit, reaching for the wine bottle as he did so and gesturing towards the glass she had abandoned earlier.

'Another drink?'

'No, thank you.'

'D'accordo…'

He angled the bottle towards his own glass then reconsidered. Not the best of ideas. So he set the bottle down again and picked up a glass of water instead, watching out of the corner of his eye as Amber's fingers drummed an impatient tattoo on the tablecloth.

'Are you going to explain that comment?' she demanded at last, evidently unable to hold back any longer. 'I need some answers.'

'In order to get answers, you need to ask the right questions,' Guido returned, taking a sip from his water glass. 'Ask what you want to know and I will answer. I will!' he added when she slanted a dubious, sceptical glance in his direction.

'OK, then—so why were you masquerading as Guido Corsentino, just a photographer?'

'I was never *masquerading…*'

His accent was very strong and rough on the word, mangling it into incomprehensibility.

'Guido Corsentino, "just a photographer", was who I was at the time.'

'That doesn't make sense.'

'Then let me explain—years ago, when we first started out on trying to rebuild the fortunes of Corsentino Marine, Vito and I made a promise to each other. We were working twenty-four hours, every day that God sent. We never had holidays, never had days off. So we swore an oath—if we succeeded as we dreamed, before we were thirty, then for both of us our thirtieth year would be free—to do with as we pleased. To stop being a Corsentino of Corsentino Marine—and, later, Corsentino Leisure—and just be ourselves, Guido and Vito. Doing what we wanted while the other one ran the business on his own.'

'And your choice was to be—just a photographer?'

'That's right. When I met you, I was at the end of my year. I'd been travelling the world, taking photographs, developing my skills, enjoying life. For the past eleven months I'd been just Guido while Vito was in charge here.'

'So why didn't you tell me?'

Guido looked into her burning, indignant eyes and drew a deep breath. Ask what you want to know and I will answer, he'd said—and he'd meant it. He was perfectly prepared to tell the truth. But there was truth and truth. Some truths she might not want to hear. And some truths he was not at all sure he was prepared to risk her knowing.

'The truth…' Amber put in now, giving him the uneasy feeling that she had watched his face and been able to read his thoughts as they went through his head.

'The truth? I didn't want to.'

But don't ask why, he added in the privacy of his own mind. That was something he was not prepared to reveal. Not yet—if ever. Certainly not until he knew more of what was going on in *her* thoughts.

'I'd had a year of living for myself—enjoying myself. No pressure. No publicity—no *paparazzi*…'

Looking into her face, he saw that she understood *that*. He could also see the shiver that had taken her body—probably as she remembered the afternoon outside the church.

'I'd promised myself that full year and I wanted every last second of it. I hadn't counted on meeting you and I hadn't counted on…*on your demands for an immediate wedding*. If I could have had things any other way, I would have done. But you were so insistent it was that way or nothing. So I went along with what you wanted—I just didn't tell you everything about myself.'

At the time he'd been happier that way too. At least, he'd believed, she had wanted him for himself. Not like so many other women before her who had looked at him and seen money signs in their eyes. That had been until she'd met Rafe St Clair.

'So why…?' Amber began again, but Guido held up his hand to silence her.

'My turn,' he said abruptly. 'You asked your question so now I get to ask one.'

That was fair enough, Amber had to concede. There was no way she could fight against it, even though there was so much she still wanted to know. She really couldn't believe that Guido would answer anything she asked.

Anything she dared to ask.

'Your question?'

He took so long to respond that her mouth dried while she waited. She wished she hadn't refused that glass of wine now as she slicked her tongue over parched lips, hoping to ease their discomfort.

'Why didn't you ask that question last week? Why leave it until now? You found out the truth about me when we were at the airport. So why hold back since then?'

Because I was scared to ask, Amber answered him in her

thoughts. Because I was afraid that if I did I'd find out more things I didn't want to know about the way you'd deceived me. Lies that you'd told me.

But in the end she'd come face to face with those lies anyway. Or with other, different lies. She knew now why Guido had married her—he'd been painfully blunt about that.

If I could have had things any other way, I would have done.

It had been her own need for a wedding, her insistence on getting married at once, as soon as they possibly could, that had trapped her. And of course he had only come to find her again in order to break up, not her attempt at marriage but *Rafe's*.

'Why?' Guido pushed when she concentrated on her thoughts instead of the answer he wanted.

'Isn't it obvious?'

She aimed for airy carelessness and missed it by a mile. Instead her words sounded brittle and heedless, making him frown dangerously.

'Not to me.'

The way he pushed back his chair and got to his feet, prowling round the room like a sleek black panther pacing its cage, only added to the sense of discomfort that was tying every nerve in Amber's body into tight, screaming knots. Her brain was spinning so that she had to struggle to bring her thoughts under control, organise the facts into some order so that she could find a way to answer him without revealing more than she wanted him to know.

'Well—well, it doesn't matter any more, does it? It doesn't matter who you are or who I am. We're only married because we have to be—because circumstances have forced us together again. We rushed into that stupid, crazy farce of a wedding a year ago when—when neither of us meant it, neither of us really wanted to be married to each other *for life*! And now—when we should be moving on, when we should both be thinking of new lives, new futures—we find ourselves trapped again.'

'Trapped?'

The word had the weirdest intonation, one she couldn't begin to unravel. At one moment it sounded as if he was questioning her feelings about their marriage, asking if she really felt that way. But at another it seemed that he was refuting her words, furious that she should put her words into his mouth. But someone had to say it. Someone had to take their courage in both hands and come out with the terrible reality of all this.

'Yes, trapped! I know you don't want to be here with me and I sure as hell don't want to be with you.'

Not like this. Not knowing that he didn't love her. That he had only come after her for revenge…

'You were right—in my bedroom this afternoon…'

'Right about what?' Guido demanded when she choked on the words, unable to get them out.

He was standing beside the window now, shoulders hunched, hands pushed deep into his trouser pockets. And because of the subdued lighting in the room, the way he was silhouetted against the glass pane, she could see nothing of his face. He was just a dark, featureless shadow, his face giving her nothing to go on, no expression to read. Nothing to give her any clue about what was going on in his mind.

Perhaps it was better this way. At least because of this, she could see nothing that would distract her; nothing that would deter her from saying what had to be said. She wouldn't be tempted to try to persuade him that it didn't have to be this way. Or, even worse, actually be weak enough, desperate enough, to plead with him, to beg for another chance. If she could see his beloved face then she might just be desperate enough to say she loved him so much she'd take what little was offered for as long a time as he would let her stay. And when he tired of her, when he wanted to throw her out, she would go without any further protest.

'Right when you said that we don't want to get caught that

way ever again. Sex just complicates things. We did it once and that just delayed the divorce we both want.'

'That afternoon was a mistake.'

'I know! It was the worst possible mistake we could have made. We don't want this marriage, either of us, and it's best if we end it now.'

She didn't know why she paused. It wasn't as if she expected him to say anything. There wasn't anything he could say.

He hadn't wanted the marriage in the first place. He'd only come back to her to get revenge on Rafe St Clair. He wasn't going to turn around now and say she had it all wrong. Beg her to stay.

He didn't, of course.

He just stood there, a dark and silent silhouette against the wall and waited and watched as she fumbled for the words—the last words she would ever say to him.

'So I think it's best if I go. If I pack now, can I still leave tonight?'

'Of course.'

It was so calm, so matter-of-fact, that it rocked her world.

'The jet will be at your disposal. If you're quick, then you'll probably be able to travel with Vito...'

Strangely, appallingly, a note of wry amusement crept into the beautifully accented voice.

'If I read my brother correctly then right now he's packing too—planning on leaving for England just as soon as he can.'

He was making it easy for her, she knew. Why should he want to hold her back when he'd had what he wanted from her? So now he was simply letting her go without fuss. And for that she supposed she should be grateful.

The only thing she could hope for now was to get out of here with her head held high and some sort of dignity intact. She wasn't going to beg—she'd gone down that road this afternoon and the rejection he'd meted out to her had almost destroyed her.

She wouldn't beg again.

'If you could just do one thing for me…'

Somehow she managed to impose a vicious control over her voice so that it was calm and desperately quiet, showing nothing of the terrible struggle for restraint that was going on inside her.

'Name it.'

'Can you order a car to take me to the airport and then leave me alone? Don't be here when I come down again.'

'I'll do that,' he said flatly. 'Of course.'

She longed for one last look at his face, one last chance to see those stunning features she adored. To imprint them on her memory for the time when memories were all she had. But Guido stayed where he was, still hidden in the shadows, and there was no chance of that.

There was no chance of anything more.

Except to say, 'Goodbye Guido.'

And to turn and start walking towards the door, out of the room and out of his life.

CHAPTER FOURTEEN

WAS he really going to let this happen?

Guido could only be grateful for the darkness of the shadows in the corner where he stood. At least that way his face stayed hidden and there was no way that Amber could see the effect that her actions were having on him.

She couldn't see the way he had to clamp his mouth tight shut to hold back the words that fought to escape. She wouldn't see the tautness in his jaw, the burning sheen in his eyes.

It was happening all over again. She was walking out of his life without so much as a backward glance and it was so much worse than the last time. The last time he had come back to the hotel room and found it empty. Found that she had gone.

This time he had to watch her go. And he felt as if she was tearing his heart apart as she went.

But he wouldn't call her back. She would hate it if he did. Because she felt trapped with him. Trapped in this marriage. And, loving her as he did, he couldn't imprison her in a marriage that was the last thing she wanted.

What she wanted was her freedom. And that was the gift he could give her, so he would make it easy for her. He would order the car as she'd asked.

Pushing himself into movement, he snatched up his jacket

from the table, hearing the faint rustle of paper in the breast pocket as he crushed it in his hand.

And that was when he remembered.

Remembered what he had brought with him tonight so that he was prepared in the worst-case scenario. Well, this was the worst-case scenario. So now—

'Amber!'

She hadn't got far, barely halfway across the hall. And she stopped so suddenly he could almost have sworn that she was waiting for his call. And just for a moment he allowed himself to hope.

But when she turned back to him and he saw her face then he cursed himself for being a fool even to let himself dream.

There was no sign of welcome, no sign of warmth in her face. It was as cold and pale as ice, her eyes just dark, mossy pools, blank and unresponsive. She didn't even speak, just stood there silently, waiting for him to say why he had stopped her. Waiting for him to tell her what he had to say so that she could go and get on with her packing.

Get out of here as quickly as she could.

'You'd better take this…'

Rigid control kept his own features taut. Once he gave her the document then that really was it. She would have no further reason to stay and he would have no excuse left to keep her.

'I saw my *avvocato* this afternoon. He drew up the papers…'

His solicitor?

Amber had found it hard enough to control her reactions in the first place. She'd jumped at the sound of his voice, turned almost before she'd realised. Because the truth was that she'd been longing, praying to hear him call her name. And she'd given away just how much she had wanted it by the speed of her response.

Her heart had jolted up into her throat, beating a frantic tattoo that stopped her breath, made her gasp in shock and disbelief as she saw him coming down the hall towards her.

And then cold reality had clamped down on her when he held out the long white envelope and said that he had seen his solicitor.

Somehow she managed to keep her hands from shaking as she pulled out the thick wedge of papers, forced her attention onto them. It was easier that way, at least, than looking into Guido's face when she'd told herself that she would never see him again.

'What…?'

The question died away to a miserable croak as she focused on the documents she held, knowing in an instant what they were.

He had even gone to the trouble of having them written in English, just in case she couldn't get the message in Italian.

Divorce papers.

Twice she opened her mouth to say the words. Both times her voice failed her, her throat so clogged with tears that she couldn't get a sound out.

Divorce papers.

Guido was saying something but she couldn't hear him through the buzzing inside her head. Her eyes closed, her hands clenching on the papers she held, she forced herself to listen.

'If you're to have your freedom then you'll need these. I had him draw them up so that you could choose the way you want to work this. I wanted to make it easy for you.'

He drew in his breath harshly and let it out again on a deep, deep sigh and because her eyes were closed she heard that sound so much more intently. So intently that she could have sworn there was a rough edge of raw emotion on it. Almost as if…

'You decide the grounds you want for our divorce,' he said. 'Anything. And I'll provide you with the evidence.'

'Anything?'

Amber barely had the strength to whisper it. She couldn't believe what she was hearing in his words—no, behind his words. Something in his tone that was threading through every syllable he said and turning it into something else entirely.

'Anything. Irretrievable breakdown of marriage—unreasonable behaviour…'

'Adultery?'

She said it blind, keeping her eyes tight shut, not daring to risk looking into his face in case she was wrong.

The silence that greeted her question was so total that she almost felt as if a block of ice had enclosed her, shutting her off from all the world. But Guido was still there, beside her. She could feel his warmth, pick up the intensely personal scent of his body. But she couldn't hear a sound.

And that gave her the courage to open her eyes and look straight into his face. Straight into the dark, burning bronze eyes.

And what she saw there gave her even more courage than before.

'Will you give me evidence of adultery, Guido?' she asked, her voice stronger, clearer, more confident. 'Will you sleep with another woman so that I can cite that in our divorce case? Will you make it easy for me that way?'

She thought she had her answer before he spoke and her heart lifted at the way that his bronze gaze slid away from hers and struggled to look anywhere but at her.

'Guido?'

'You cannot ask that of me,' he said at last and his voice was as rough and hoarse as if he was suffering from a desperately painful throat. 'Not that. I will do anything but that.'

Once more her voice deserted her as she tried to answer him and on a jolt of distress she saw him turn away again.

'I'll get the car organised.'

'No!'

Because of the effort she had to make to force it out, her denial was so much louder, harder than she had ever intended, making him swing round in consternation.

'No,' she said more softly but more confidently. 'The car can wait. I don't think we've finished talking.'

'We haven't?'

'No. I find I have a couple more questions I need to ask you. And you said that if I asked, you would answer. Is that still the case?'

There was a wary look in the golden eyes, one that made her think of a cat tensing, ready to jump if someone made the slightest wrong move. She could only pray that what she had to say was not that sort of mistake.

'Ask,' was all he said. No guarantee that he would answer.

She'd start with the easier ones first.

'When we were married—in Las Vegas—why do you think I left you?'

'Because you didn't believe our marriage was legal. And because Rafe St Clair came along and—to quote the letter you left behind—he was a much better choice for you. He could give you more of what you wanted. And, knowing about your mother, I guess I can understand why.'

If hearing her own bitter words quoted back at her wasn't bad enough, then Guido's understanding made it far worse. It was all Amber could do to force herself to speak again.

'It wasn't his blue blood or anything like it that made Rafe appeal to me,' she said, choosing her words carefully, needing to get them just right. 'He—he said he loved me.'

'Loved!'

Guido's bark of laughter was the most brutally cynical sound that Amber had ever heard and it made a sensation like a rush of ice-cold water run right down the length of her spine, making her shudder uncontrollably.

'St Clair never loved anyone except himself.'

Whatever else was true, one thing was certain: Guido detested Rafe St Clair with a vengeance; she could have no doubt about that. But had that hatred been the only reason why Guido had arrived to break up her wedding?

'So why did you come to England a week ago?'

The look he shot her was one of frank disbelief.

'You know why. To stop a bigamous marriage.'

'Just that? So what about that need to get revenge on Rafe?'

She'd taken a step too far, too fast. His head came up, rejection stamped on his stunning features, bronze eyes flashing a warning.

'You heard that?'

'I heard.'

He clearly wasn't pleased that she had overheard that part of the conversation but where before his dark, frowning glare would have had her backing down, now she saw it as a defensive gesture, a shield up to hide something he was far more worried about her knowing.

'What have you got against Rafe? What did he do to you?'

For a long, fraught moment she didn't think that Guido was going to answer but then he drew in another of those long, deep breaths and let it out again slowly, hissing through his teeth.

'He seduced and bankrupted my cousin. Took what he wanted and then walked out.'

Blunt and spare as it was, it was something of a slap in the face. She'd actually started to believe that this revenge story was a pure red herring. That he was using it as a cover-up. But it seemed that after all there was some substance to it.

So had she been wrong all along?

'Well, I'm sorry that she ended up with a broken heart...' She began, her voice uneven and unsure.

'He...'

'What?'

'*He*,' Guido repeated so firmly and clearly that she couldn't mistake it. 'My cousin Aldo is male.'

'Are—are you telling me...?'

'My cousin Aldo is gay. So is Rafe St Clair.'

'But...'

Amber's legs were suddenly like cotton wool underneath

her, making her stagger where she stood, her hand coming out for support. Immediately Guido was at her side, his arms going round her waist, holding her upright.

Held like this she was right up against him, her face just inches away from his, green eyes looking up into burning bronze. There was nowhere they could look but at each other and Guido showed no sign at all of wanting to dodge away this time.

'Rafe—is *gay*?'

It seemed impossible to believe. But now, looking back, she could see things she hadn't taken much notice of before— things she had actually liked, been thankful for, He had been so very restrained where sex was concerned. He had said she could set the pace for them, that he could wait until their wedding day. His kisses had been gentle, his few caresses tentative, almost gauche. But she had been thankful for that. Bruised and battered by the wild, fierce storm of her passionate relationship with Guido, she had seen Rafe's apparent consideration as a calm, safe haven where she could rest, lick her wounds and recover.

'But why would he want to marry me?'

'Because if there's one thing that Rafe loves as much as himself it's the estate. And he's hidden his sexuality from his parents for years now. There's a reason for that. If his father knew the truth then Rafe would never inherit. Lord St Clair wants a married heir to succeed him—grandchildren to carry on the family line. He's been putting pressure on Rafe to provide both. I've no doubt that Rafe thought he would be able to convince his *padre* that his marriage to you was genuine. He might even have resolved to consummate it—anything other than the truth being found out. I couldn't let him do that to you.'

To you. Did he know how much he'd given away with that?

It was time for her to make some move; to show him something of how she felt.

'I have to thank you so much for that.'

She looked deep into those burning eyes as she spoke and it was only when Guido's shoulders dropped that she realised how tightly they had been held, tension stiffening his big body. She almost smiled then, relief breaking through her own apprehension, but she had to hold back. They still had a way to go and anything could go wrong.

'Even though it trapped you into a marriage you didn't want?'

'You' again. Guido was still only talking about her. Looking back with clearer eyes, she now saw how throughout the whole of the evening he had never ever said anything but 'you'. She had been the one who had claimed that they had both felt trapped—and she knew in her own heart that she had been lying about herself.

Taking a deep breath, she gathered her courage to speak.

'We both locked ourselves into this marriage. That afternoon was mutual, what we both wanted—what I wanted. What I still want.'

Because he was holding her so tightly she felt the shudder that ran through the whole of his body. And she saw the flicker of reaction deep in his eyes.

'So now…' She lifted the papers she still held so that they were there between them. 'Tell me about these. Tell me about the grounds for divorce you'll give me. Tell me why you're prepared to work at proving irretrievable breakdown or unreasonable behaviour but you won't take the obvious, the simple way out and let us use adultery as grounds to end this marriage.'

'Because…'

Just for a moment Guido hesitated. He closed his eyes for a second but when he opened them again they were clear and bright and strong and filled with an emotion that made Amber's heart leap in hope.

'Because when I made my marriage vows, I meant them in good faith. I vowed to love, honour, cherish—to be faithful to my bride. And I meant to keep those vows. So even if the marriage is ending there are some things I cannot do and one of them is that I cannot be unfaithful to the woman I love.'

I cannot be unfaithful to the woman I love.

What more could she want? What greater declaration did she need? Tears sprang into her eyes but they were tears of joy. And her heart raced so fast that she thought it would burst out of her chest.

But all she could say was, 'Oh, Guido! Guido!'

And that was not enough. She had to get control of herself. Had to say something more. Guido needed more. He deserved more. So much more.

'I—I don't want you to have to do that either,' she managed shakily. 'I want this marriage, Guido. I always have.'

And then the full impact of what he'd said burst in on her. The whole, the wonderful truth about his declaration of love.

'You said when—"When I made my marriage vows, I meant them in good faith"—even then...'

Her mind was whirling in so much delight that she wasn't making sense. But Guido didn't need her to explain any further. He knew exactly what she was trying to say.

'Even then,' he echoed, the faint smile that curved his mouth tugging so hard at her heart. 'When we made those vows in that tacky little wedding chapel. Even if they were made without a real blessing, or my family around, I meant them—for life.'

'But—but you said that...'

'That I didn't want to get married—I didn't—or I thought I didn't until I met you. And that wedding was not at all what I wanted...not for you. When I married the woman I loved I wanted it to be the biggest and the best wedding she'd ever wanted. I wanted to invite my family and friends—the world. I wanted everyone to see how happy I was, how lucky to have this wonderful, beautiful woman as my wife. But that wasn't what you wanted.'

'I was scared...'

She could admit it now.

'I was so in love with you, but I was terrified that if I didn't hold you to me—get you to marry me—then one day I might wake up and find I'd lost you. I rushed us into that tacky wedding…'

Her sigh was deep, full of regret for the way she'd let things go wrong, for the time they'd lost.

'Guido, believe me—that day was so special to me. It was the biggest and the best wedding I'd ever wanted because I was marrying the man I loved. But I was so afraid that you didn't really love me that I convinced myself it was true. I made it happen…'

'No.'

Guido's hand came up to her mouth to stop her words.

'No—I never stopped loving you. Even when I tried—I never could.'

'And neither could I.'

She spoke against his fingers, loving the scent of his skin so close, the taste of him against her lips.

'I thought I did—but I was running away. Running from the fear, the belief that I just wasn't right for you. I was still running when I said yes to Rafe. I thought I could hide… But I was wrong. So wrong.'

'Amber…'

Guido's voice was so deep, so lovingly intent that it made her senses swim. She could look nowhere but into those dark, dark eyes, seeing in them the love she needed; the love that had always been there but that she hadn't been strong enough to believe in until now.

'I love you, Guido,' she said, all the confidence of her convictions ringing in the words. 'I love you and I want this marriage—our marriage—for the rest of my life.'

She barely got the words out before his mouth came down on hers in a kiss that was so fierce, so intense, so passionate that it made her head spin. But at the same time it was a kiss of such gentleness, such giving, such caring that it brought tears of joy to her eyes. It was a kiss that held all the elements of Guido and his love for her. A kiss secure in the love they shared.

When at long last they parted, Guido moved slightly away from her but only enough to enable him to see her upturned face. Stroking her hair back from her face, he looked down into her eyes, his smile wide and strong and gloriously happy.

'Amber, *amata, carissima*—my heart is yours. I'm yours for as long as there is breath in my body. I know we are already married—and you said that the wedding we had was all you wanted—but…'

The laughter in his throat was soft, warm, in a way she had never heard before.

'But I'm a man—a Sicilian man! I still want the world to know that you're mine. I want to stand up in front of my family—my friends—and say that I love you and I want you for my wife.'

'Then we'll do it,' Amber told him. 'We'll have that special day—we can renew our vows, start afresh, begin our married life all over again.'

And this time she would have no doubts, no fears, no insecurities that would get in the way, she told herself as he took her mouth in another passionate kiss. Guido loved her and she loved him and that was all she needed.

'There's just one thing…' she whispered as that kiss heated her blood in her veins, her heart rate kicking up several beats, her breath coming faster. 'This wedding ceremony—we don't have to wait…'

'Wait?'

Guido sounded horrified at the thought and the thickening of his voice told her all she wanted to know. His hands swept down over her body, caressing every inch of her with an ardent, knowing touch—a lover's touch.

'There'll be no more waiting,' he assured her. 'Never again. We are man and wife—and I intend to prove that to you right now.'

Lifting her off her feet, he swung her up into his arms and carried her down the hall—heading for the stairs. And through the thudding pulse that made her blood pound in her head, Amber knew one thing with the total, unhesitating confidence of truth.

This time really was the start of forever.

Men who can't be tamed...or so they think!

Damien Wynter is as handsome and arrogant as sin.
He will lead jilted Sydney heiress Charlotte to the altar and
then make her pregnant—and to hell with the scandal!

If you love *Ruthless* men, look out for

THE BILLIONAIRE'S SCANDALOUS MARRIAGE

by Emma Darcy

Book #2627

Coming in May 2007.

BRIDES OF CONVENIENCE

Forced into marriage— by a millionaire!

Read these four wedding stories
in this new collection by your
favorite authors, available in
Promotional Presents May 2007:

THE LAWYER'S CONTRACT MARRIAGE
by Amanda Browning

A CONVENIENT WIFE
by Sara Wood

THE ITALIAN'S VIRGIN BRIDE
by Trish Morey

THE MEDITERRANEAN HUSBAND
by Catherine Spencer

Available for the first time at retail outlets this May!

Introducing talented new author

TESSA RADLEY

*making her Silhouette Desire debut
this April with*

BLACK WIDOW BRIDE

Book #1794
Available in April 2007.

Wealthy Damon Asteriades had no choice but to
force Rebecca Grainger back to his family's estate—
despite his vow to keep away from her seductive
charms. But being so close to the woman society once
dubbed the Black Widow Bride had him aching to
claim her as his own...at any cost.

On sale April from Silhouette Desire!

**Available wherever books are sold,
including most bookstores, supermarkets,
discount stores and drugstores.**

REQUEST YOUR FREE BOOKS!

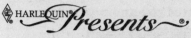

2 FREE NOVELS PLUS 2
FREE GIFTS!

HP07

From the magnificent Blue Palace to the wild plains of the desert, be swept away as three sheikh princes find their brides.

When English girl Sorrel announces she wishes to explore the pleasures of the West, Sheikh Malik must take action—if she wants to learn the ways of seduction, he will be the one to teach her....

THE DESERT KING'S VIRGIN BRIDE

by Sharon Kendrick

Book #2628

Coming in May 2007.